Easy Riders:
The Older Ones

David Xu

Copyright © 2020 David Xu

All rights reserved. No part of this book may be reproduced or transmitted in any form or by any means, electronic or mechanical, including photocopying, recording or by any information storage and retrieval system without permission in writing from the publisher. This book is fiction and opinion. Many views in this book do not reflect those of the author. All characters are composite.

Mountain View Press—Ashland, Pennsylvania
ISBN: 978-0-9999035-2-0
Library of Congress Control Number: 2020925543
Title: Easy Riders: The Older Ones
Author: David Xu
Digital distribution | 2020
Paperback | 2020

On the cover:
The author's 2013 Harley Davidson Breakout with a paint job like Wyatt's bike in the great 1969 movie Easy Rider (Captain America's bike).

Other books by David Xu:

Easy Eddie Books I, II, and III,
Redneck Dystopia, and
Orphans in The Barn

Dedication

This book is dedicated to my wife, family, friends, and bikers. They say that you do not choose your family, but I would choose this bunch every time. Some folks are hard to love. I definitely fit that description. Three decades in the Army can make a person grumpy. Soldiers are not paid to be nice. I am still working on that.

We had the best times as kids running wild and riding hogs together from Apopka, Florida to Danville, Virginia. The family is a gold mine of material. Nancy, the wife, is sweet, loving, smart, sexy, and strong. She keeps me going day and night.

I also dedicate this book to all the good bikers. They are the quintessential Americans who love America's history, work hard, and cherish Christian values. They are strong, successful and love capitalism and freedom. Many bikers give their time and money to help the less fortunate with toy runs and other activities.

Most bikers love limited government and maximum freedom as per our awesome constitution. They will not tolerate socialism, communism, dictatorship, and love our three equal branches. Most bikers love to shoot guns and have a great time. They work hard and play hard. They stand and salute the beautiful United States of America flag. I thank God and Jesus for my wife, family, friends, and bikers. Bikers know that freedom is not free. God bless the awesome, capitalistic, strong, and free United States of America!!

Contents

Dedication v

Introduction ix

Chapter One: *The NYC Score and The Plan* 1

Chapter Two:
Rolling Through PA, MD, West Virginia, and Virginia
.... 41

Chapter Three: *Cruising Around in NC and SC* 89

Chapter Four: *Rocking Down the Highway in Georgia*
.... 126

Chapter Five: *Rumbling Through Alabama and Mississippi* 158

Chapter Six: *The Old Bikers Enjoy Louisiana* 190

Introduction

I have always had a fascination with motorcycles. Growing up in Florida, we had the good fortune that our older sister Betsy had a boyfriend with a Benelli minibike. He taught us how to ride and that is all it took to be hooked for life. The biker understands why the dog sticks his head out the car window and looks so happy.

We never dreamed as kids that we could afford the big and beautiful Harley-Davidson. It was a bridge too far. We were lucky to afford playing cards to tape onto our bicycle forks to make an engine noise. The hog is usually shiny and loud. It shakes the rider and the road for a great experience in freedom. The biker lifestyle and twisting a Harley-Davidson throttle are exhilarating.

This book is about two older guys and their ladies taking the road trip of a lifetime on their hogs in the spirit of the road trip in the great 1969 movie Easy Rider. Many bikers and non-bikers dream of the huge road trip and the excitement, freedom, and surprises that come on the road every day in America. Many bikers never have the time, good health, and money simultaneously to actually take that awesome trip.

I have always loved rock and roll music. The lyrics are hilarious if you can understand them. I watch interviews of rockers explaining how they wrote great songs and the meaning behind the songs. There is something magical about very talented people yelling, playing drums, picking guitars, and bass guitars together. I included many references to rock songs in this book to celebrate the awesome musicians.

Does that make sense? Now stop reading this mediocre book immediately and crank up "Easy Living" by Uriah Heep, "Lazy" by Deep Purple, and "Rock Candy" by Montrose. Get the cobwebs out. That is your rock and roll homework before reading this masterpiece.

The biker loves the sense of danger and living on the edge. They understand risk and reward and how to maximize joy. He or she rides from dark places into the bright sunshine and blue sky. Hardcore bikers love to scrutinize and chat about any Harley-Davidson motorcycle. It could be a $4,000 used Sportster, a $44,000 new Touring CVO Limited, or anything in between.

Nancy and I have met the nicest folks at Daytona Bike Week, the Laconia Bike Rally, and the Sturgis Bike Week. We love to walk around and check out all the bikes. Main Street in Daytona is a blast. Lake Winnipesaukee is big and beautiful. The Black Hills are amazing with all the short trees. There is always great food around too. The odd and funny bikers are the best.

I hope you enjoy this awesome biker trip that does not involve drugs and very little alcohol. Dan and Ford will take great care to avoid all brothels on their epic ride. They have fun riding hogs with their ladies clinging to their waists. Nobody dies on this ride.

You will meet many odd, good, and funny bikers in this book. I hope you get excited while opening this book. I hope you feel like crossing the bridge into Daytona Beach during bike week. Americans and foreigners have fun together in the land of milk and honey on these pages. Live to ride and ride to live!

Dave

Chapter One
The NYC Score and the Plan

Dan's Day Dream Sequence from the summer of 1980.

The party is just getting going. It is midnight somewhere near Turbeville, Virginia. "Born To Be Wild" by Steppenwolf is playing on the massive stereo and speakers. One hundred high school and college kids have taken over Kenny's parent's house while they are out of town to party. The music and laughter are loud. Kegs of beer are flowing. The scent of pot is in the air.

Dan and Tommy arrive just after midnight on their shovel head Harley-Davidson motorcycles. They are loud with straight pipes and a lot of chrome. They spend every spare dollar on more chrome. They are half drunk from the previous party that night. Dan pulls up and does doughnuts around the bonfire. He tears up the grass and dirt and rocks are flying. The other students love it and cheer him on.

The house is a two-story with a covered front porch. Wild high school and college students are everywhere talking trash. The muscular boy on the wrestling team stuffs the small boy into a trash can for entertainment. The small boy has a big mouth and must be punished. "You Ain't Seen Nothing Yet" by Bachman-Turner Overdrive is playing.

Cathy and Kelly are chatting next to the bonfire. Cathy is chubby and a great student. Kelly is pretty, popular, and a poor student who does not like reading books.

"I could not sleep last night and I realized something. I am going to read every book I can get my hands on. It is fine for you to date the guys and have a great time, but I am taking a different path. I will follow God, Jesus, and learning forever," Cathy said.

"That is fantastic, but I feel a need to date David after Mark at some point. Tonight may be the night. Let us just have a good time and things will work out," Kelly said.

Cathy knows that the key to great success and happiness for her is to learn everything she can, get a great job, and then find love. She will rise to great heights with this plan.

The loudmouth kid is lucky to avoid a swirly. That is when several guys dunk someone's head in the toilet and flush as punishment. The girls are trying to decide which boy to date. Boys are hanging out of the upstairs windows yelling at girls. The two acre yard is surrounded by tall pine trees. Some couples are making out and planning their next steps for the evening.

Dan's best friend Dennis is smiling ear to ear next to the bonfire because he just pulled off the roommate switch and is arm in arm with Kim. He dumped Amber for shoplifting and picked up Kim. This was a huge upgrade in quality and looks. It is estimated that 95% of roommate switch attempts fail. Amber stole a bottle of wine and some cheese at the Trump Winery when they attended the concert last week and that was the last straw. The security guard caught her and she is headed to the slammer for the third offense.

"Feel Like Making Love" by Bad Company comes on the stereo. Dennis is singing along and thinking about his new squeeze and how grand his life is now. His situation changed for the better in a New York minute.

Dan rides his 1979 Super Glide with drag bars and sparkled blue paint job. Tommy rides his black 1971 Super Glide with drum brakes, peanut fuel tank, and raked out front end.

He spray painted the bike brown for two reasons. Number one is that money is tight. Number two is to be funny with an ugly, plain, and brown Harley. Who does that? Both bikes leak oil, but look and sound fantastic. Harley quality suffers under the AMF buyout and ownership from 1969 until 1981. The bikes are long and low. Only six boys can afford Harley-Davidsons at the huge high school in Danville, Virginia.

One kid chokes on a chicken bone from laughing too hard. Tommy is evaluating the ladies for attractiveness and receptiveness to his awkward advances. He is weak with the small talk, but his muscles are big and the girls dig it. His girlfriend just dumped him for cheating and loving his Harley Davidson more than her.

"Let that be a lesson to you," Tommy said to the kid choking. He always says that. The boy at the parent's stereo plays "Tush" by ZZ Top. He ran speaker wire out the front door of the house to the bonfire to crank up rock and roll on the massive speakers. The parents love the Lawrence Welk show and have many vinyl records from it. They will notice blown speakers and scratched records when they return from Myrtle Beach on Monday.

Sandy, the cutest girl at the party, is checking out her boyfriend Dan. She likes what she sees on the hog and joins him for a hug and kiss after his antics on the bike. She has the body of a gymnast with perfect calves. She has long brown hair and a part-time job at Christmas as Santa's elf in the mall. Dan likes what he sees too.

Sandy will ride home with him tonight. Dan will cut the engine and coast to her house so her sleeping parents will not hear the roar of a Harley. They would be mortified to know that she is dating a crazy biker and/or riding on a Harley. Her parents assume she is with other high school girls in Daddy's car.

Back in the real world, the Javitts Center in Manhattan is packed with motorcycles and wild bikers on three different levels. The largest bike show in the United States is underway. It is the end of July 2020. The bikers love it, but many people thought the show would be canceled due to the Corona virus from China.

Ford and Dan are identical twins from Danville, Virginia. They lived far apart for many years and now live in the same village in coal country. They ride motorcycles all the time and live in Ashland, PA. They drove to NYC today in Ford's huge diesel F-250 Ford truck for the event. It is red and he loves the turbo acceleration by the massive engine. The engine is so big, it has two batteries to crank it.

The two men are from the same egg and very patriotic. Dan pulled thirty years in the Army and Ford loves business and capitalism and had his own home improvement business for many years. Ford grew tired of paying a lot in taxes and inspects buildings for the state now. They both realize that the United States is the greatest nation ever to grace the face of the Earth. They try to buy American-made products when they can. They love Harley Davidson motorcycles.

Dan and Ford love just roaming around checking out the bikes and freaks at bike shows or anywhere. They sip coffee and have snacks and chat about Harleys and everything. They meet at their farms and the local Harley Davidson shop in Orwigsburg, PA all the time to ride and have fun.

Come To Papa by Bob Seeger comes on the stereo. The brothers play air guitar and drums while they enjoy seeing so many custom Harley-Davidsons. Rock and roll is the favorite genre with this biker crowd.

They will ride anywhere to see other Harleys and get nice meals. They walk around inside Bill's Bike Barn in Bloomsburg every few months. He has vintage bikes, cameras, hobby horses, and other odd stuff in a huge warehouse. Admission is $5 paid to the wife. She only takes cash.

The last time they walked around at Bill's, they saw a balding man with a funny tattoo. It was a man pushing a lawnmower tattooed on top of his very bald head. It looks as if the character is mowing the hair on the sides of his head. The biker is a walking cartoon strip.

Both of them have a fixation with dental care and with flossing. Ford likes the floss pick that is Y shaped. He keeps twenty in his pockets at all times. Dan prefers the traditional spool of floss and always has some. Dan and Ford are 58 years old now. They will walk, talk, and floss in any situation. Others stare, but these two bikers do not care much what others think. They realize that they are just two old, oddball bikers who have it made. Money is not a problem after decades of financial planning and hard work.

They both bought used 2013 Harley Davidson Breakouts back in 2014 and love the fat tires, wide front end, and softail frame. This model just looks right to them with the fatbob fuel tanks and drag bars. They would not be caught dead on a Japanese bike covered in plastic. It just does not look right. American steel is the only way to go. How weird is it to think that Harley-

Davidsons were made in Japan before World War Two? They pay cash for everything they buy to avoid paying interest to greedy bankers. This includes houses and vehicles.

Both bikes have the official Harley turbine chrome wheels. They each have 21 thick spokes made of bright chrome that reach out to the edge of the wheel. The wheels looks like huge diamonds to them.

Dan's hog is painted with an American flag on the gas tank and chrome fenders. Dan and Ford love the classic movie Easy Rider from 1969. Dan loves the Captain America bike ridden by Wyatt. Ford painted his Breakout like the other bike in the movie. It is painted orange and red with yellow flames like the other bike in the movie ridden by Billy. The have watched Easy Rider clips many times and love the silly conversations between the bikers and the rock and roll music.

Peter Fonda and Dennis Hopper made the movie about the 1960s counterculture and riding from California to Louisiana on beautiful Panheads. They encounter fun, discrimination, and sorrow along the way. Mardi Gras is a blast and then tragedy hits on the way back home.

"Do you remember what the Amish construction team leader told us in Lancaster that day at Cracker Barrel? Elam King told us that birds of a feather flock together. He was most certainly right. The bikers love to hang together," Ford said.

"I just remember how big and strong his hands were. He was so strong and full of wisdom. Everything he said was so profound," Dan said.

They say that engaging in an activity that requires total concentration is a good way to stay happy. This keeps the negative thoughts at bay. These two guys firmly believe in that. Riding hogs is the definition of freedom and exhilaration to them and requires total concentration.

"Check that guy out. I wonder how many tattoos he has?" Ford said to Dan.

"Do you know who that is? That is the nut with tattoos covering 200% of his body," Dan responds.

"Wow! Now that is dedication to the art form. I saw him on TV a few weeks ago in a documentary about the Sturgis bike rally in South Dakota. He goes every year. Have you seen the governor out there? She is hot and would get my vote for anything. She is a good Republican," Ford says.

"That governor is the best. On the other hand, the tattoo guy is a freak for sure. Just think about his ultimate stupidity. He has tattooed his entire body twice. I wonder what Bee would think about that," Dan wonders.

Bee is Dan's charming wife. She is a tiny Chinese-American woman with a biting sense of humor. Bee, Dan, and Ford do not take crap off anyone.

"I would love to know what percentage of his tattoos are the result of alcohol and/or drug binges. You could not be sober and pay someone good money to do that to yourself. I wonder if he paid for all those tattoos. Perhaps he was in prison for a long time and bored," Dan said.

"I bet the true answer is somewhere between 99% and 100% of the tattoos on that bloated and disgusting body were done while he was drunk or high. What do you think about that bike?" Ford said.

"Very nasty! What was she thinking? I bet it would be hard to sell," Ford said. The bike is purple with a custom paint job. There are wizards, unicorns, and rabbits all over the fat bob tanks and fenders. This is one of the custom bike shows in the convention center. It is a Harley Davidson Super Glide from 1979.

The two twins took different paths in life for sure. Ford worked in construction for many years and now inspects buildings for the state of

Pennsylvania. Their drunken father followed the same career path and loved Ford trucks. He named his second son after the Ford truck. Ford was married and divorced twice and single now. He has a heart of gold, but does not take anything from anyone. He can never fully take his eyes off the ladies.

Dan is a farmer and retired from the Army after thirty years of service. He is married with one son on Long Island. The son works hard and is very successful. His wife Bee grew up in China and is very direct with her communication. They all love God and Jesus and have a great time getting high on life.

"Do you like wearing that mask?" the stranger said to Dan as he and Ford are looking at motorcycles.

"No, not really, but I am afraid of getting the virus," Dan replied.

"You know you don't have to wear it. The corrupt and stupid politicians just want control. Just take it off," the strange biker said.

The stranger is wearing a tank top with a lot of hair and fat hanging out. He is not wearing a mask out of protest. Most folks wear a mask and try to stay six feet apart to avoid getting sick or making others sick from the Wuhan virus.

Dan and Ford quickly walk away from the aggressive and ugly biker who is trying to harass people who wear masks. It would be pointless to argue with such a fool.

"Wow! That is a nasty and ugly little man. He must weigh 300 pounds. He looks like an orangutan," Dan said.

"He looks like a tick or the penguin character in the Batman movies. You know he really resembles the grotesque KSM (Khalid Sheikh Mohammad) when he was arrested. Now he was a fat, hairy, and horrible creature," Ford said.

"I bet the US Seals grabbed KSM right out of bed for that mug shot. I bet he would love to have that photo back. His hair was messed up and he did not have time to tweeze his omnipresent chest hair or change out of that disgusting t-shirt. Did you notice he was staring at me before trying to shame me? I tried not to notice or look at him," Dan said.

"Yes, his eyes were wide open before he said that stupid crap. I wonder why he thinks like that or does not think before he speaks. I bet Osama and his friends laughed at KSM's mug shot when it came out during 2003," Ford said.

"Do you know they waterboarded that fat idiot 183 times at the CIA black site in Poland?

He spilled the beans after that episode. I wonder if he ever lost the weight," Dan said.

"I wonder if he tried to have happy thoughts during the interrogations. I close my eyes and think about dogging the Breakout rolling down the highway whenever the dentist causes me pain. The happy thoughts help me get through the pain," Ford said.

"I fantasize about the CIA agents waterboarding you whenever you subject me to your boring thoughts and stories. That helps me get through the pain. Your tales are brutal to get through. You really need some new material," Dan said.

They see all kinds of bikers. One guy had on a space suit from the Star Wars movies. A woman wore a bra as a top. Many biker women wore leggings. Some bikers have tattoos on their heads and faces. Many wear leather tops, chaps, and pants. Funny tales are told using poor grammar and perfect grammar.

Large-breasted women sit on brand new motorcycles in order to manipulate some dumb bikers with bad credit. The young ladies wear short shorts and tight t-shirts for the customers. Highly effective salesmen lurk nearby to close the deals. Many bikers will pay up to 22% interest on these motorcycle loans for years or until the repo man comes.

About ten bikers line up on a big stage in the corner of the hall to try pole dancing. A DJ from a radio station and a stripper from the Discotheque Lounge in Augusta, Georgia help the contestants. The DJ informs the crowd that there is a movement to get pole dancing into the 2020 Olympics. It has been postponed due to the Wuhan virus until July 2021 in Japan.

"Layla" and "The Core" play on the convention center sound system. The kid running the sound system cranks it up for Eric Clapton and company.

The fit nurse is laughing too much to be successful. The chubby construction worker has some success, but the pole is moving around too much. The man makes everyone laugh. The real estate agent has been training on her strip pole in her basement for months. She wins the contest easily and $200.

The brothers speak with many nice folks. Most of the bikers are nice and friendly. They love to talk about Harley-Davidsons and riding. They love to joke around. They love a good snack or meal. They discuss new parts for the bikes and clothing for their rides. Many ask for advice on how to make their hogs faster.

Two actors from the old Dukes of Hazard TV show are signing autographs. The line must have thirty bikers in it. The actors smile, but look burned out and tired between conversations with the bikers. The redneck car steals the show. The assistant to the stars tells a biker that this is the car that Bubba Watson bought for $110,000 back in 2012.

Ford and Dan walk out of the convention center and walk toward the subway station. They hear shouting by protesters. BLM and Antifa members and supporters are out in force. There must be hundreds of them here in Manhattan.

Protesters and counter-protesters yell at each other. The protesters want socialism and more free stuff like apartments, food, and health care. The counter-protesters tell the other side to get jobs and shut up. The two bikers are concerned for their safety and walk briskly to the subway station at Penn Station.

The brothers go into a McDonald's and buy thirty cheeseburgers. They walk into an alley and pass them out to homeless people sitting on the sidewalk, smoking cigarettes, and dozing. They do this sometimes and it reminds them of being young boys in church and how the Bible teaches everyone to always give back to the less fortunate.

Dan and Ford both made a ton of money buying dilapidated houses and selling them. The IRS gets no tax if you live in the house at least two out of the last five years. Many folks do not know about this way to make tax-free money, but the brothers learned this at an early age and worked hard with it.

They take the south train to Battery Park and catch the Staten Island Ferry to get back to Ford's truck. Four guys dance and sing on the subway for tips. They lack any talent and receive few tips. Dan and Ford drove over for the bike show for the day and parked at the ferry on Staten Island. The ferry is free and the parking lot is gigantic.

"Check out this bumper sticker. Now that is a good one," Dan said.

The bumper sticker says "Get Your Dick Beaters Off My Truck" next to a cartoon depicting a hand.

"Who would put that on their vehicle? Who makes these crazy bumper stickers?" Ford said.

"It seems like more and more folks are angry in the good old USA. More people need to work hard and the government is too big and handing out dough so lazy folks can just sit around," Dan said.

"Yes, many people are unemployed, tired of wearing the mask, and have cash to burn from the government. This is a socialist dream," Ford said.

"Wow, that is an awesome car! What year is it?" Ford says to a young man wearing an Antifa shirt. The protester looks tired and is unlocking his spotless Chevrolet Corvette.

"It is a 2018 model. My Uncle just passed away and left it to me in his will. He was a very loving and generous business man," the young man said.

The Corvette is shiny red with fat tires and chrome wheels. Most men would love to own and drive a car like that. It looks great and is extremely fast.

"I always wanted a Corvette, but never bought one. The fiberglass body and two doors are a work of art," Ford responds.

The Corvette is the most popular sports car of all time. General Motors made them from 1953 until today. They are low to the ground and most men absolutely love them.

"Do you want to buy it? I lost my job and really just want the money. I have a clean title from my Uncle. He always paid cash for houses and cars. I want to finish college and start a business just like him," the young man said.

"I would love to buy it. Will you take $25,000 cash? That is all my budget allows right now. Money is tight my man," Ford said.

"That is great. It does have a couple scratches on it and I do not need a flashy car like this," the young protester said.

"Why are you out protesting? It is good protesting weather. I have never protested anything. We just vote for the person who wants less government," Ford said.

"My friend knows a big fat union boss and he pays us $10 per hour cash. We have to wear the approved Antifa shirt. It is an easy gig. I guess he would get mad if he knew that I support capitalism and just want a job right now," the young protester said.

"That is alright. How did you hurt your arm? Were there counter-protesters out today? Did the police get you?" Dan asks.

"Oh, this cut, no, I cut it with the weed eater yesterday. My mom makes me mow the grass and cut the weeds every week. She is a good mom," the protester said.

"This kid is going to be alright. He is a hard worker," Ford said as he slides him $100 for being a good kid.

The two exchange contact information and Dan and Ford climb back into the truck for the

160 mile ride home to Pennsylvania. The protester lives in the basement of his parents' house on Staten Island. They live on Victory Boulevard.

"Do you know how much that car is worth? You got the deal of a lifetime," Dan said to Ford.

"I know, I know. That fine automobile is worth at least $50,000. It is a limited edition. I saw that model in my Corvette picture book that Phil found at Ollie's. He kept one and gave me one. He is the best neighbor," Ford said.

Ford drives back with a rollback truck the next week to pay for the car and take possession. Dan travels with him on a lazy Monday. Both of them smile and laugh all the way from Ashland to Staten Island thinking about the fantastic transaction on this beautiful vehicle. Ford jumps on this great deal on the car.

Ford puts the Corvette on Craig's List and sells it within a week for $50,000 to a dentist from Pittsburgh. The dentist is fat and bald and having a mid-life crisis. The car is a perfect fit for this guy.

The two brothers ride hogs from Ashland to Tamaqua to celebrate the deal with a great meal at a Hibachi restaurant. They call in the order because there is only outdoor seating due to concerns about the virus from Wuhan, China.

They have fun rolling up Highway 81 at 80 mph. They take turns passing each other and dogging their powerful machines. The truckers and drivers in cages watch the crazy bikers having fun.

A guy in a U-haul truck is having a bad day. Another driver will not let him cut into traffic in a construction area. The U-haul driver is so mad he flies into road rage with his eyes bulging out of his skull. He is honking the horn and giving evil looks at the other driver.

The dumb U-haul driver finally has to hit the brakes and wait his turn to flow into the one-lane stretch of highway. He has always struggled with planning ahead. They say the drunk plans for Saturday night and the successful person plans for generations.

Dan and Ford pull into the strip mall parking lot where the Hibachi place is located. The walk around and talk about their big and beautiful Harley-Davidsons.

"Did you notice that the government folks in Shenandoah put up their Christmas lights already downtown? It is nice, but their decorations are dirty and worn out. That village has seen better days," Dan said.

"No, no, that old mayor over there did that. Did you know that she is 80 years old now?

They leave the Christmas stuff up year round as a budget cut. She said that it saves $10,000 in tax money each year to do that. Those union government employees are expensive. I bet they vote against her every four years," Ford said.

"That is top rate government work. Do you know that she owned a sweet Panhead back in 1960? There is a great picture in city hall of her sitting on the hog on Main Street in Shenandoah during a bike rally during the summer of 1960. She has always had that beehive hairstyle and was in great shape. She has smoked a pack of cigarettes per day and gone through five husbands now. I would vote for her for anything," Dan said.

I know that is true. She has a huge Harley-Davidson tattoo on her left bicep. What a woman! She should be president or governor," Ford said.

A man is sitting on the curb and up to his elbow in his nose searching for gold. He cannot extract the debris or boulder and is visibly frustrated. He stares at the sky with his mouth wide open. The bikers notice that he has on an employee outfit from the Hibachi restaurant. He works there.

"What shall we do? We already paid for the meals. He probably does not work in the kitchen?" Dan said.

"Are you crazy? You know he works in the kitchen. I think I saw him back there a few weeks ago. I cannot consume that food now after seeing this gross display," Ford said.

"No, no he takes the money at the cash register. I never saw him enter the kitchen. He is the money man. He and the young kid take turns taking the money," Dan said.

"Yes, but where is he when the smart kid is counting the money? I bet he floats between the register and the kitchen. How can we be sure that our meals are booger free?" Ford said.

"My bet is that our meals are free of nasal mucus. I am sure that he washes his hands after walking outside for a pick. They have signs to remind the employees about sanitation," Dan said.

"Do you really think that the dumb and dirty employees read those signs? I bet they do not read anything at any time. He just plays video games and picks his nose. That is the complete lifestyle for this person," Ford said.

Dan wins the debate and they try to enjoy the meal sitting on the curb in the parking lot. They make light of the odd and gross situation. The picker retreats into the restaurant after dislodging the piece of gold.

"Is that a big piece of pepper? What is that different taste? Does it seem more chewy this week?" Ford asks.

"We should write an anonymous letter to the manager to ask the picker to hang out behind the strip mall or in the bathroom," Dan said.

"Let us skip that step and call the health inspection. That guy needs help. He is begging for help. It is a cry for help. They should lock him up. Why can't he just bite his fingernails like you? You look like a mental patient," Ford said.

"I asked the restaurant owner how old his son is at the cash register a while back. He said that he is 10.6 years old and his daughter 12.4 years old," Dan said.

"Wow, that is wild that he thinks and speaks in decimals. I guess he does not care for fractions," Ford said.

"That is what he said. He likes decimals better than fractions. That is the way he was taught in Taiwan growing up," Dan said.

The two bikers finish their Hibachi steak meals. The food tastes good, but they worry about the nasal debris and the unhygienic employee. They walk around for a bit and floss their teeth. They walk around and analyze each other's bikes. Every nut and bolt fascinates them. They discuss how the factory workers assemble the bikes in York, Pennsylvania.

They each leave a $20 tip for the server and then wonder if the other one left a tip. Both brothers are great tippers. They have tipped like crazy for several years since making a lot of money. They thank God for enjoying so much success. A stranger walks up to have a look at the shiny motorcycles.

"I love that paint job. Is that like the Captain America bike in Easy Rider?" the stranger asks.

"Yes, I always loved that movie, but not the part about drugs. Ford's bike is painted like Billy's in the movie. I love the flames," Dan said.

"The riding scenes are awesome with those hogs. You can tell that they are riding at a slow speed for the filming. That Toni Basil looked good as a lady of the night at the end," the stranger said.

"Oh Mickey you're so fine you blow my mind. Hey Mickey! Hey Mickey! I love that song. It is catchy. She wears too much makeup in the video though," Ford said.

"Did you know that she is from Philadelphia? What is funny is that she was really a cheerleader in high school in Las Vegas after the family moved out there. That was a great part of the music video," Dan said.

They chat for a while and then hit the rode on the chrome Harley-Davidsons. Ford leads the way to go back home on country roads. He prefers two-lane rural roads instead of highways. He enjoys the view more that way.

The farmers look up from their crops when they pass by. The road and ground rumble from the loud engines and exhaust pipes. Even the Amish farmers enjoy watching the bikers go by. They call the hogs painted horses.

They stop for gas at a local and small service station. Three old guys are sitting on the liar's bench telling lies and enjoying some coffee. They walk over to check out the bikes glistening in the sunshine. Ford tells the girl at the register that she is doing a great job and gives her a $20 tip.

"What is this for? Thank you so much! I was just worrying about money since my boyfriend moved out. I have a little boy. That piece of crap found another woman. Thank you so much," the cashier said.

"Did I tell you about the old Amish guy who built our house in Harrisburg? His hands are enormous and strong at 80 years old. Those Amish are master craftsmen and did a great job," Dan said.

"Yes, I remember he was big and strong and said if you had a conflict that you would handle it the way they do in the Bible. You would get a friend or family member to arbitrate and avoid the greedy lawyers and judges," Ford said.

"Boy, you have a great memory. The old Amish team leader told me that when he was a kid his neighbor had a Harley. He took the kid for a ride and came by the Amish farm at 60 mph. The Amish kid's father told him later that he would never do that again," Dan said.

"I read that many young Amish leave their village for the real world to see what it is all about. Most of them return and stay in the village for life. You have to respect that," Ford said.

The two old and odd bikers ride to the local Harley Davidson shop in Orwigsburg. They love to talk to the owner. She is a very nice widow. She and her husband started the dealership back in 1967. He died a few years ago and the bikers loved him. Nana and her son Dennis are so nice and strive for excellent customer service.

Dan and Ford park their hogs in front of the dealer and notice an old and dirty man sitting on the liar's bench. His name is Bob and he sits there often. The building has a huge covered porch and big windows on the front side. It is a great place to sit and shoot the breeze.

"That is a nice bike. What year is it?" Bob asks.

"It is a Breakout from 2013. I loved the Easy Rider movie if you can tell," Dan said.

"That is very nice. I enjoyed the silly conversations in that movie. I guess you have money. I don't have any," Bob said.

"Where did the money go?" Dan inquires.

"I never had any. My parents have money, but not me," Bob explains.

Dan gives Bob a $50 Harley Davidson gift card to be nice. Bob cannot believe his good luck and buys a nice shirt. Dan and Ford walk into the showroom. The new motorcycles fascinate them with more and more technology and power.

"This is the new Heritage Softail. It lost 40 pounds from last year's model. They lightened the frame with stronger American steel and went from two shocks to one," Phil the salesman said.

Phil is short with a full head of hair and a Dutch accent. He owns a Sportster and a Deluxe and loves to hunt. He gives his coworkers beef jerky and steaks from the big animals he shoots. He is big on dental care.

"That is amazing. I love the way the engine has four spark plugs instead of two. I will upgrade in a couple years. My wife and I just buy used stuff with cash now that we are older," Dan said.

"What is the best seller regarding color? I bet it is red," Ford asks.

"Believe it or not, black is our best seller. Bikers still love the black bikes. My wife loves the purple motorcycles with sparkles. She is a Peter Pan super fan," Phil said.

Ford walks into the bathroom. There is a small sign or sticker on the wall behind the toilet that reads "Weight Limit 500 Pounds." He wonders who came up with that specific weight. How many bikers are close to that weight? Do they have a problem with toilets caving in or falling through the floor?

The two chat a while about the new bikes with Phil and then walk over to say hello to the owner.

"Hello Nana! How are you doing? I tried to make the family day event, but had to work," Dan said.

"Hi there. We had a good time. Several friends and family members told some good stories about Tom," Nana said.

Tom is her deceased husband. Once per year the dealer has family day. There are vendors, a band, DJ, authors, and food trucks. Toward the end of the day anyone can grab the microphone and tell a funny or sweet story about Tom and Nana or anything. It is a great time for all.

Dan and Ford walk outside and Bob is still relaxing on the bench smoking a cigar. He loves to talk to strangers. His wife left him a long time ago.

"The world is going down. I don't know what is happening. There are too many bad people," Bob said.

"Well you make a good point. We are doing what we can. The price of bread is outrageous. Keep it real. Have a blessed day," Ford said.

"What the hell does that mean? Oprah lost 50 pounds," Bob asks.

"It was just a joke. I was just trying to be funny. See you later," Ford said.

The two brothers ride motorcycles down Highway 61 to Cabela's for lunch. Ford loves the bison burger. Dan likes to walk through the museum with 200 stuffed animals.

"You know we should celebrate my financial upturn. Let us take a long ride," Ford said over lunch.

"That is a fantastic idea. Where shall we ride? I have never taken a really long ride. Let us go for it brother," Dan said.

"I always wanted to ride to Key West, Florida. Wife number two and I flew down there a long time ago and it was nice," Ford said.

"I will ask Bee if she minds if we go. Just two odd bikers from Pennsylvania on the road just sounds right. Perhaps New Orleans would be fun. Is the trip on you?" Dan said.

"I did not say that. Just joking. Yes, the trip is on me. You are a lunatic on a low budget," Ford said.

Ford pays for the meals with cash. The total is $26 for both of them. He gives the young man at the register $50 and walks away.

"Mister, you left your change. Your change is $24," the young, honest man said.

"Twenty-four dollars is change," Ford said.

"I got that one from Frank Sinatra. He used to tip and say funny things like that," Ford said to Dan.

"Bungle In The Jungle" comes on the stereo by Jethro Tull. This band with Ian Anderson playing flute is awesome. Not many rock bands have a flute player.

"Very nice! You are so loaded now. Perhaps you can purchase some awesome HD clothes for me or maybe more chrome for my baby. Do not hide it, but divide it my sweet and generous blood brother. We are very close now," Dan said.

"Yeah right! This bison burger is the best. What is the difference between bison and buffalo?" Ford said.

"Buffalo are indigenous to Asia and Africa and bison are from North America and Europe," Dan explains.

"I wonder if the meat tastes the same. I bet it does not. Those tourists in Yellowstone just cannot seem to stay away from the bison while taking the selfies. A woman was gored again last week out there," Ford said.

"I find your belief system fascinating," Dan said. The brothers get many bits from the Seinfeld show.

Dan and Ford finish their meals and walk around flossing. Some of the stuffed deer were shot 60 or 80 years ago. They look so fresh in the display. Even their noses still look wet or moist. Taxidermy has come a long way. There are wildebeests, lions, tigers, elephants, and many other dead animals on display.

They see a large woman wearing black leggings with bright red roses on them. Her t-shirt reads "I may be fat, but you are ugly. I can lose weight."

"I would love to talk with her. I bet she has one heck of a sense of humor," Dan said.

"Yes, that is hilarious. Good people," Ford said.

The brothers love music. They love rock and roll music the most. Their conversations turn to the sweet memories of some of the concerts they attended back in the 1970s and 1980s. The ZZ Top song "La Grange" plays in the store.

"Do you remember that KISS concert in Greensboro back in 1978? I think that was our first big concert," Dan said.

"Yes, those were good times. That guy started a fight over that girl I made out with. I had to fight off him and that other girl," Ford said.

"I remember you punching the guy and the girl. She had long fingernails and jumped at you," Dan said.

"I took care of business that night. I think it was during the encore," Ford said.

"Yes it was. I will never forget seeing you and that girl experiencing free love on the beer soaked concrete floor of the Greensboro coliseum. That was hilarious," Dan said.

"Those were good times. I remember seeing Ted Nugent jump around in the loincloth and ZZ Top and Blackfoot. We saw Van Halen with David Lee Roth and Sammy Hagar," Ford said.

"That show with Bon Scott and AC/DC was awesome and them with Brian Johnson was great too. Angus Young in the school boy outfit spinning around on the stage floor is burned into my memory," Dan said.

"I know. The tickets seemed so cheap back then. We did not have nay dough. The concert tickets now are astronomical," Ford said.

"Do you remember the cops sweeping the parking lot in Roanoke before the Heart concert? They arrested hundreds of young and wild kids. The bought concert tickets for nothing. They arrested Jay for pot and he had to spend the night in jail," Dan said.

"That was hilarious that his cellmate urinated on his pants while he was sleeping. He was stinking the next morning when we bailed him out. I remember that we had tickets to see Aerosmith in Greensboro, but the singer got sick. That was a big disappointment," Ford said.

"I just remember that we did not have enough money for the Jethro Tull tickets in Raleigh. That sucked. The guy played flute in a rock band," Dan said.

"We saw the Outlaws, Poco, and Mother's Finest too. Being roadies for Mother's Finest in Danville, Virginia was the best. The band members were so friendly," Ford said.

"You know I had most of those concert tickets in a cardboard box in my basement a few houses ago. I remember being stressed out from packing and moving and throwing the box in the trash. That was really dumb," Dan said.

"That sucks. It would be so great to put them under glass and hang them on the wall in your house. I bet the price for each one was about $12," Ford said.

"I remember you were drunk and frisky and made out with Kelly in my back seat. She had already vomited on the way to see John Mellencamp. That was very nasty. You had very low standards my man," Dan said.

"I know it was an embarrassing situation the next week at school. She was so aggressive and horny after she vomited. I guess we both just smelled like alcohol. She did look good though," Ford said.

"You really belong in a cage. You are like a gorilla or orangutan. Are you always going to be like that?" Dan said.

"No, no, I have changed. Life is good and I behave now for the most part. That was the alcohol talking my brother. I am like a monk now," Ford said.

Bee and Dan drive to Harrisburg to the International Market. She loves to find exotic foods from around the world that she used to enjoy growing up in China. Dan has to be dragged to the place and gets bored.

She finds products and puts them into the cart. He takes the products out, reads the label, and tells her why she should not buy them. They consume some wild stuff around the globe.

"Century egg from Thailand? I do not think so. This crap was preserved in clay and ash. Did you know that King Rama X married his first cousin and has a harem of 20 concubines? We cannot support that. This egg stinks like sulfur or perhaps ammonia," Dan said.

"There is no way I can eat these organic adzuki beans from China. They look like pellets from a deer's butt. Did you read that Papa Xi is rolling back the freedom for the poor Hong Kong people? He looks like a turtle that lost its shell. He is very nasty. The British had the colony over there for some reason, but that is over. The beans are very low of saturated fat (none), but I cannot eat this," Dan said.

"Black pudding from Swaziland? There is no way we are buying bloody sausage from these people. That horny, obese King Mswati picks a young girl from the big parade every year and makes her his wife. He is out of control and too gross and frisky. Why can't you get the certified sausage from North Carolina? That fool has 15 wives now. Any more than 10 is ridiculous," Dan said.

"These tuna eyeballs from Italy have to go. You would be interested to know that their former Prime Minister Berlusconi loved prostitutes like Ruby. That is bad enough, but he called them bunga bunga parties. I guess the me-too movement only applies to America," Dan said.

"Chicken feet from Uganda? Idi Amin made all the Asian people leave the country because they were too good at business. Do you really want to be a party to that? Do not get me started on all the poor folks he executed or ate for lunch. Idi was a big, big boy with a voracious appetite," Dan said.

"This licorice from Libya has to go. Did you know that Gaddafi was addicted to Viagra? Think of all the beautiful women who had to pretend to like that ugly dictator. He hit on the wives of foreign dignitaries also with that horrible cigar breath. There is no call for that," Dan said.

"You cannot purchase this Russian pickled cabbage. I still cannot get rid of that image of Putin on the horse without a shirt. He is very nasty, but he does have that rhythmic gymnast going for him. It appears that he removed his chest hair by the roots. He looks like a seal or maybe a mole," Dan said.

"This roasted and seasoned laver looks divine, but it hails from Korea. What the hell is laver anyway? I am sure that President Park was up to no good hanging out with that cult woman. They impeached her for that crap you know. The staff at the Blue House said she abandoned some puppies. That story must be true," Dan said.

"That is delicious. Have you ever tried laver? It is red algae from the Yellow Sea. It is very yummy," Bee said as she snatches it from Dan's hand.

"Go sit in the car. You are not right. People eat different things in different countries. Please be normal. That woman heard you," Bee said.

"I am not your dog. I will not sit in the car like your German shepherd. I caught a whiff of the seafood section. That must be really bad. I think I saw a squid climb out of the tank and stroll down the aisle toward the vegetables. The butcher was trying to kill it with the broom," Dan said.

Dan walks around thinking about and singing a song by Jane's Addiction "Been Caught Stealing." He loved the video about dumb young guys stealing stuff in a grocery store. His friend George used to do that when they were in high school in Danville, Virginia. He would make a ham sandwich and eat it while browsing in the grocery stores and never got caught.

A large woman in a green top and black leggings is walking in front of Dan. She is talking to her boyfriend on the phone on speaker. She is telling him what they will do the next time they are intimate. He mentions another girl's name. Her stomach is hanging over her belt and sagging.

"Do you have another girlfriend? I do not mind. I just want to know. It is okay. I just do not want to argue with you baby. Three is a good number," the woman said to her boyfriend.

Dan thinks back to his youth and how things have changed. If he had made that mistake, all his girlfriends would have dumped him cold. He surmises that this new generation is out of control and has no boundaries.

Dan noticed this woman going through the check out lane when he walked into the international market. She bought only one item for consumption during her shopping trip. He thought it was odd to only buy one item while everyone else in line bought many items. Her t-shirt reads "Harley Girl."

She eats Spicy Chili Crisp from a glass jar from China. She always brings a spoon from home for this activity. The ingredients are; soybean, onion, monosodium glutamate, and pepper powder. The jar has an odd picture of a scowling woman with a man's haircut on the front. This is the spice of life. This is the good stuff.

Dan walks in the strip mall. The sign on the Lane Bryant reads "DO NOT ENTER if you are experiencing or have experienced symptoms of COVID-19, such as fever of 100.4 Fahrenheit or higher, chills, cough, shortness of breath or difficulty breathing, fatique, muscle or body aches, headache, new loss of taste or smell, sore throat, congestion or runny nose, nausea or vomiting, or diarrhea."

He wonders who owns or runs this place. Boy, they are really into writing warnings. A rabid group of lawyers must own the place. Or perhaps the owners are afraid of their own shadows. Do any of these symptoms lead to dramatic weight gain? That could help sales for sure. They are too paranoid about headaches. Does anyone read this crap? What a crazy world this is with a virus floating around.

He observes two older men arguing at the cash register. The employee apparently was rude to the customer and an argument ensues.

"You are welcome? Why should I thank you? You should thank me for shopping here. What is wrong with you? Do you realize that my shopping here pays your check?" the shopper said.

"You could have thanked me for helping you buy the products. You are a chunk of doo-doo. I bet you like Trump," the employee said.

"Who uses the word doo-doo anymore? I kind of like it. I miss that word. You are a piece of crap. How does that word fit you? You are 100% fecal matter. You are a big chunk of excrement. You look like a dung beetle," the customer said.

"You look like human waste in the toilet that is stringy and resembles a strand of DNA," the employee said.

"Cease fire. You are extremely creative with your insults. Thank you so much. Now go take a shit. You look bloated. Have a blessed day," the customer said.

Bee and Dan see a yard sale sign that amuses them. It is on a telephone pole on the way home in Frackville. There is no telling what the folks in coal country put up on signs. It reads as follows, "Yard Sale: Toys, Knives, Legos, Cartoons, Car Seat, Guns, Baby Stroller, socks: A Family Event."

Chapter Two
Rolling Through Pennsylvania, Maryland, West Virginia, and Virginia

Dan and Ford are rolling down Highway 81 on a bright and sunny morning. They pulled out of Ashland this morning at 0900. Dan wanted to get on the road earlier, but Ford enjoys sleeping late.

Ford listens to rock and roll music while riding his hog. Dan listens to the roar of the engine and wind while riding his hog. Dan thinks it is a little bit dumb and unsafe to listen to music while riding a motorcycle. He harasses Ford for fun.

Ford is listening to the Marshall Tucker Band in his full shield helmet. The song is "Take the Highway." Both brothers wear huge helmets with face shields for safety. That makes more sense to them than mounting a huge windshield on the Harley. That just would not look right.

They are cruising at 80 mph passing through Harrisburg when they see a large woman on a trike. She has a tank top on with short shorts. She has a spider tattoo on the top of her foot. She is riding down the highway with no helmet and without shoes on.

She is married and divorced several times. A huge unicorn is tattooed on her left shoulder. As the bikers pass her, they notice that she is jerking her head back and forth checking them out in her mirror. They give each other the thumbs up.

The bikers stop for a cup of coffee and biscuit at the Speedway gas station next to the highway. They pull the chromed-out hogs up next to the outdoor tables in front of the huge gas station. Some college boys are getting ice bags from the freezer while holding cases of beer. They check out the Harleys and tell Dan and Ford how nice the bikes are.

"Did you see that beast on the trike? She gave us the thumbs up. I think she wanted some," Ford said.

"I think you are just right for her. She is hilarious riding around without the helmet and shoes. I bet she would be a fun-loving woman for you. It will hurt that head if she wipes out though. She must protect her brain," Dan said.

"Thanks, but no thanks. She has no brain to protect. I have my hands full now. The food bill would be tremendous with her around. She looks like she has been rode hard and put up wet," Ford said.

They two enjoy the coffee and bacon, egg, and cheese tacos and talk trash. The coffee is not as good as when they had Dunkin coffee at these stores.

"This is the first time that I have tried the Speedway coffee. It is really not that good. This reminds me of the awful coffee in the army," Dan said.

"I know. I loved the Dunkin coffee here. I asked the cashier if it was any good when we paid," Ford said.

"Well, the reviews have been mixed," the chubby cashier said. He has on a Def Leopard t-shirt. He has "I Want You To Want Me" by Cheap Trick cranked up on the store stereo.

"Have you seen the new Dunkin Donuts signs? I can imagine the meeting in Canton, Massachusetts when the guy in the back came up with the idea to burn millions of dollars to change all their signs," Dan said.

"I have a great idea for the business. Let us change all the signs to remove the word "donut." This will be hot, trust me. That word is trouble. People want healthy fare and donut means fat and unhealthy," the dumb guy said at Dunkin Donuts headquarters.

"Wow! That is a great idea. I never thought about it like that. People will buy more donuts if we DE-emphasize the word donut. Perhaps we should sell healthy salads too," the CEO said at the board meeting.

"Can you imagine how many donuts they have to sell just to pay for all the new signs? Did someone complain about the donut word? Who cares about the new, improved signs? I just want good coffee and donuts," Ford said.

An older couple are sitting under an umbrella at the table next to Dan and Ford. They are having an intense discussion in low voices, but the bikers can hear everything they say while they are chewing.

"You cannot move back in. There is no way that will happen. You really hurt me when I saw you with Brenda. She is so gross. I cannot believe that you like her," the woman said.

"But baby that was just temporary. She means nothing to me. That happened so long ago. She was the aggressor. I am really a victim in this situation," the cheating man explains.

"It was only last week you dumb ass. I really trusted you and let you use my car all the time while I was at work. You did not even help pay my rent," the woman said.

"Oh baby, you know I will be good this time. Let us make up and watch some TV at your place. I am outdoors you know," the man said.

"I know you are homeless, but maybe that is where you should be if you will not work hard. Perhaps that is who you are. I cannot trust you anymore. Goodbye," the woman said. She walks away leaving the cheating man to sip his coffee, finish his danish, and contemplate where he is going to stay tonight.

Dan and Ford look at each other and smile and laugh. This is very interesting to see this couple break up. It seems like he cheated on her last week and now they are meeting at a neutral place to discuss the horny man's behavior and punishment. He wants to try again, but she is tired of his cheating butt.

"She made a good call to dump this frisky man. She reminds me of the girl you dated in high school. Was her name Pam?" Dan said.

"Yes, I dated Pam for a while in 10th grade. She was sweet and always had a wad of money from her father," Ford said.

"What was her nickname? Slimy thighs? I wonder how you earn that nickname," Dan said.

"I always felt that she did not deserve that nickname. She did not get around that much," Ford said.

"Are you joking? She serviced the entire football team. She did look good though. You were the bad and dumb boy," Dan said.

They finish the mediocre tacos and coffee and walk around flossing and checking out their bikes and a couple others that come and go. The American flag gas tank is shining so bright on Dan's Breakout. Many bikers and non-bikers admire the yellow flames and red background on Ford's Breakout also. The chrome fenders blind you when you walk by the bikes.

Dan and Ford are very proud of the bikes. They love the fat tire on the back, plethora of chrome, and custom paint jobs. The bikes are worth $20,000 each. This is a dream trip of a lifetime and they know it. They have both worked hard for decades and now it is time to play hard together.

Dan calls home to chat with Bee in Pennsylvania. She always jokes that if he goes on a good trip without her to not call her. She threatens to get a young boyfriend.

"Hi baby. How are you? I miss you," Dan said.

"I am fine. What do you want? I told you to not call me. My boyfriend and I are busy here discussing our feelings. He is very manly unlike somebody," Bee said joking around.

"We just had some nasty breakfast tacos and suspect coffee at Speedway in Harrisburg and I was thinking about you. I miss you baby," Dan said.

"Really? That bad food is good enough for you. Are you having fun? Is your butt sore?" Bee said.

"Yes, we are having a ball and my butt is sore. We just walked around the parking lot and flossed for a good while. We just listened to this couple breaking up sitting next to us. He cheated and she refused to take him back. It was so funny," Dan said.

"She made the right call. I would do the same if you cheated. I am not like the wives of the frisky politicians who take them back after they cheat all the time," Bee said.

"You are brutal. You should love me even if I make a mistake. We all have limitations," Dan said.

"You have so many limitations. Okay, would you do that if I got a boyfriend?" Bee said.

"Well, perhaps you are correct now that you put it that way. I love you sweet baby," Dan said.

"I love you too. Have fun and be safe. Don't call me," Bee said.

"We will watch some rock and roll documentaries and concerts when I get home. Would you like to see the old and ugly men perform some classic rock songs singing about picking up young ladies?" Dan said.

"That is disgusting to see the wrinkled rock and roll men singing about picking up young women. I do not know why you like to watch that. Those skinny 60 and 70 year old singers dancing around look so dumb. It should be banned," Bee said.

They use the bathroom and walk some more and then hit the road. Ford takes the lead and dogs his Harley getting back to the highway. Dan loves it and tries to keep up. They are free with plenty of dough in the awesome land of milk and honey known as America.

They ride down Highway 81just enjoying the sound of the hogs. Ford listens to "Flirtin' With Disaster" by Molly Hatchet. The band's name refers to a prostitute who allegedly killed her clients. The traffic is light and moving along between 70 and 80 mph. The vibration of the handlebars feels great to these brothers.

Ford points to his gas tank so Dan knows he is pulling off for gas. He forgot to fill up when they stopped for breakfast. He got lost in cleaning his chrome and wheels.

They ride through Carlisle. The houses are old and small. An old man with a long beard is walking down the city street and gives them the thumbs up. There is a billboard that says "We are in this together. Fine Jewelers."

They see another billboard that reads "We are here for you. Smith Hospital Group."

They stop at a local gas station. It feels great to walk and talk and just take a break from the noise and vibration.

"Did you see that billboard? It should say "We are in this together. We are over here in this expensive neighborhood and you are in the bad neighborhood because you are lazy, but we are in this together," Dan said.

"Yes, it should say "We are kind of in this together. Please give us your money for this over-priced jewelry and we will be over here for you in our big house, but not close by with you in your dirty, tiny apartment," Ford said.

They think it is funny when people with money pay to advertise and say dumb things like that. Many folks have been laid off during the pandemic and others have plenty of money. That is the nature of life and capitalism. It is the normal course of life with good and bad and ups and downs.

These two brothers believe that hard work will get you through the good times and bad. They firmly believe that following the Bible and God and Jesus is the best way. Dan volunteers by driving old veterans to the VA hospital in Lebanon and Ford delivers food to poor folks with Meals On Wheels. They have a dark sense of humor, but have big hearts and give to charity all the time.

"Did you know that Jim Thorpe went to college here? He was awesome with the gold medals at the 1912 Olympics in Stockholm, Sweden. He was an Olympic lover and daddy too with three wives and eight rug rats," Ford said.

"I know he was strong like a bull. The International Olympic Committee (IOC) took his medals because he played semi-pro baseball like so many others. Thank goodness, the IOC dumb dumbs restored his medals in 1983," Dan said.

"Old Jim had trouble with money and the bottle. He had some interesting jobs such as ditch digger, security guard, bouncer, actor, American Indian chief, and movie extra. I wonder what his major was in college. I wonder if he learned anything in college," Ford said.

"I cannot imagine having eight children and no money. I wonder if he was just really horny or just loved his genes very much. He must have really loved his genes," Dan said.

The brothers pull out of the gas station and round the block. The city streets are lined with two story brick buildings. There are jewelry stores, drug stores, and real estate agents on Main Street.

Most people are wearing masks to avoid the virus and staying six feet apart. Some folks walk out into the road to avoid breathing the exhale of others. A minority of people do not fear the virus and take no precautions.

Nobody imagined this weird reality until 2020. The Chinese should have contained this horrible virus, but let it spread around the world. One old man is wearing his best tie and has a windshield and a mask on for supreme protection. He forgot to zip up his pants this morning while preparing the virus protection gear.

They hear and see a siren behind them after just leaving the downtown area headed toward Highway 81. It is a Carlisle local policeman on their fenders. They are proceeding at 40 mph in a 40 mph zone.

"How long have you had your license plate? You know it is supposed to be mounted with the letters and numbers horizontally or left to right," the cop said.

"I have had the tag a while. I thought is was okay to mount it vertically," Dan said.

"It is hard for officers to read it that way. I am giving you a ticket for improper equipment," the officer said.

The rookie cop smiles and drives away. He does not have common sense and should be focusing on the real and violent criminals instead of harassing bikers.

"Boy, he was a jerk. Bikers are all over Pennsylvania with their tags vertical like yours. Anybody can read it that way," Ford said.

"I know. I asked a couple local cops around Ashland if this is okay. They said that only a dumb, rookie cop would give a ticket for that. The tag looks better that way," Dan said.

"Well you found your dumb rookie cop for sure. Let us ride like the wind brother and get away from this idiot," Ford said.

The brothers stop by the Army Museum to stretch their legs. There is a gravel path that leads around old helicopters, tanks, and sandbags. They see a man sitting on the park bench sticking q tips up his nose and into his ears.

"Look at this lunatic. He must be practicing for his Covid-19 test. Maybe he is just cleaning house," Ford said.

"Perhaps he enjoyed the virus test so much that he sticks stuff up his nose all day long. That is the weirdest habit I have ever seen," Dan said.

"No, no, do not forget Jim Green in high school lighting his farts with a cigarette lighter. I could not believe that farts are flammable," Ford said.

"Oh yeah, he would lay on the floor and stick his butt up in the air and do that. He was a showman for sure," Dan said.

Dan and Ford proceed down Highway 81. There is a huge paint can beside the road. It must be 20 feet tall and 15 feet in diameter. It catches your attention for the paint store. They notice that the paint can sign is fading and really needs painting.

There is an adult video store beside the highway. The owner put up fencing around the parking lot so local people cannot identify other locals patronizing the place. The place has strippers and erotic DVDs for sale.

The farmer pays for a huge billboard next to the strip club that reads "Sinning is of the

Devil." This sign is between the highway and his corn field.

They ride some more and then stop for a bathroom break. The know Lowe's has clean bathrooms and are easy access without keys. Ford is waiting outside the bathroom while Dan does his business.

"Don't Fear The Reaper" by Blue Oyster Cult comes on the sound system. Dan remembers reading that the manager came up with the band name in a poem about aliens coming to Earth.

"Boy, I feel the mother load today. Come on baby," Ford says to himself, but out loud. An old lady turns the corner of the aisle and hears him say this. She smiles and walks away briskly so as to avoid any odors coming from this weird biker. She thinks he probably is dumb and has the virus.

"I wonder why the stall walls do not come all the way down to the floor. This nut next to me had his pants and belt lying on the disgusting damp floor," Dan said.

"That is very nasty. I ensure that nothing touches the floor or anything. You know a healthy crab can jump ten feet," Ford said.

"I bet you are way off with that. I just know that many times the floor is little damp and yellow in front of the toilet," Dan said.

"Wish me luck. I have the mother load ready to rock and roll. I had buttered corn last night," Ford said.

"You are one disgusting person. I will be outside with the hogs. Do not take all day. You are very nasty," Dan said.

They finish their business at Lowe's and walk around the parking lot some. It feels great to stretch your legs after being on a motorcycle for a while. Dan and Ford have some arthritis and stiffness.

They see a man arguing with an employee about having to wear a mask. The employee will not let him in the store without one.

"Boy, that guy is anti-mask. I do not mind it. It covers up many unattractive faces," Ford said.

"I am tired of wearing the mask, but we need a vaccine for the Wuhan virus. Your mask does break up the monotony of your face," Dan said.

"You know we are identical twins," Ford said.

"I realize that but, I look much younger and thinner than you my brother," Dan said.

Ford has struggled with his weight since high school. He is chubby and Dan is thin. They playfully insult each other all day long.

"You look like Michael Jackson or Prince when they weighed 120 pounds," Ford said.

"There is no way that is the case. I weigh 168 pounds. That is exactly what I weighed in college," Dan said.

"I only weigh 200 pounds and gained it when I quit smoking a few years ago. That is one reason that I still smoke. It helps keep the weight off," Ford said.

"Opray lost 60 pounds last month. How about that?" Dan said.

"I think she is anti-man and a touch racist. She really needs to buckle down and lose 150 pounds," Ford said.

"Let us find a massive steak for lunch. The t-bone is my favorite now," Dan said.

"I love that one too. My eye doctor just told me that he dated a vegan woman a few years ago. They attended a vegan conference in the District of Columbia and everyone there was thin. He converted the next day, lost 30 pounds, and then they broke up the next month," Ford said.

"Perhaps she wanted a thinner man and dropped him like a hot rock. Or maybe she wanted a real man with some fat and muscle," Dan said.

Dan and Ford jump on the bikes and pull out of the big Lowe's parking lot. Several Hispanic men love the chrome and loud bikes and stare.

They rarely see Harley Davidsons up close and want one.

They ride a while more and stop at a Texas Roadhouse for lunch. The server is a young and attractive woman. She kneels on the bench cushion with plenty of cleavage in view.

They enjoy the hot rolls and butter while waiting on the salad, potato, and steak. The server is very attentive and always get a big tip. She shares with the bikers that she is graduating from college this year with a degree in math.

"Amber is very impressive. She seems smart and works hard," Dan said.

"You hit the nail on the head with that one. I think she likes me," Ford said.

"Well, as Seinfeld said, they do work on tips," Dan said.

The brothers enjoy the steak and talk some more trash about high school memories. Dan heads to the bathroom and Ford walks outside. The restaurant is in a strip mall with many other stores. He sees a palm reader and hires her to play a joke on Dan.

"This is Jasmine and she reads palms. Let her read yours," Ford said.

"I am not doing that. It is silly. She will just spout generalities," Dan said.

"No, I already paid for you. Go in there and let her do her thing. I went to one last week and it was fun," Ford said.

She is dressed as a witch, but wearing white socks and Adidas sneakers. She must be about 70 years old with long, gray hair.

"I see another man in your future. Are you happily married? I am not sure on the timeline. Are you married to a man or a woman?" Jasmine states as fact and not opinion.

"What? Are you sure that is the secret message from my palms? I think Bee is happy with me. Let me call home and have a chat, Dan said.

"There is a pool boy near Ashland and he will come into your life soon. He has broken up a few marriages already. This is predetermined. Do you have a pool now? Be careful out there. It is a jungle," Jasmine said.

Dan walks out of the dark office wondering how she knows he is from Ashland. He finds Ford laughing hard and walking in circles. Dan realizes that Ford told Jasmine to say crazy things to him. They walk around looking into the store windows and flossing.

Dan and Ford hit the road and cross into Maryland on Highway 81. A young couple on Sportsters pull in behind them. The man is on a blue one and the woman is on a black one. They are young and in great shape. The four give each other the thumbs up and smiles and dog the Harleys.

They roll through the sliver of Maryland in ten minutes and hit West Virginia. The mountains and trees are so beautiful. Ford listens to John Denver music in his big helmet. He loves the song entitled "Take Me Home, Country Roads" by Henry John Deutschendorf, Jr., Bill Danoff, and Taffy Nivert.

Dan feels some intestinal pressure and pulls off into a huge gas station. The young couple follow Dan and Ford. Dan rushes into the bathroom while the others buy fuel.

"Did you you ride with your husband before getting your own bike?" Ford asks.

"Yes, but after a while I wanted my own bike because bighead struggles with the difference between red lights and amber lights," Karen said.

"You are rough baby. I am an expert driver and was born that way. You know that is true," Dale said.

"I thought he was intelligent in college because of the water head, but that was misleading. I guess the glasses through me off too," Karen said.

"You are one tough cookie. I bet he deserves that treatment though," Ford said.

"I have five siblings and Dale has seven so we are used to the give and take of family members. His brothers used to put him up on the fireplace mantel if he talked too much," Karen said.

"Those were tough times. I am glad Karen cannot lift me up onto the mantel now. She would definitely do that," Dale said.

Dan walks out from the building rubbing his stomach and feeling much better after having a bowel movement.

"That felt like twins. They put police tape around the bathroom until the fall. That was wet and wild," Dan said.

"You are very nasty. We can do without the bowel movement commentary odd biker. I filled up your tank with the precious 93 octane fuel. I paid for their gas too. I support any young folks who work hard. Many of them are too fond of getting our tax money for doing nothing," Ford said.

"I like that. Let us ride. Where are you going?" Dan asks the young couple.

"We are riding down to Myrtle Beach to see my mother. We had to get out of New York with the shutdowns and virus," Karen said.

"This is our exit for the country route over to Virginia. Thanks for the ride and awesome conversation. Thank you for the gas. Have a great ride," Dale said.

Dan and Ford leave the station and roll on down Highway 81 to Maryland. They switch bikes just for kicks. Karen and Dale turn the other way and head East down a country road. The brothers head to the East Coast Sturgis bike rally. It is a big event with many wild bikers in New Orleans, Maryland. The country roads to the rally are full of pot holes and dangerous.

They pull into the campground and main stage area. A thick 40-foot tree is mounted above the gravel entrance on two twenty-foot trees used as posts. "East Coast Sturgis" is burned into the huge tree. There is a State Trooper there in case things get out of hand. A big sign says "No Nudity Beyond This Point." The bikers will have some fun this weekend.

The brothers set up in their cabins and meet the owner of the farm and the biker event Ken. He is outgoing and very direct with his communication. He does not take crap from anyone.

"How is the turn out this year? I guess it will be a little slow due to the Wuhan virus," Dan said

"Well, you are right, but we have a good crowd this year. Some guys from New Jersey burned a huge sculpture that looked like the country of China last night. The beer is flowing and the women are ready," Ken said.

There is a redneck standing next to the country road with a sign that reads "Show us your Tits or do a Burn Out." He is surrounded by twenty other rednecks sitting in lounge chairs and whooping and hollering. They are very drunk on this hot afternoon. They want to see somebody get wild. An older female biker raises her shirt on the way by and gives the crowd a good shot at her left, enormous breast. The crowd roars its approval.

The brothers see many freaks at the rally. One couple has many earrings in their noses and ears with chains connecting them. They hold hands and hug 24/7. Many tattoos grace their bodies. They are soul mates and ride a yellow 2000 Road King.

A dirty biker without a shirt on rides by with a blowup doll on the back. He smokes a cigarette at all times unless he is sleeping. The doll is an official sex toy for lonely and dumb men. He dreams of having a robot doll from Japan, but it is too expensive for his budget right now.

An obese insurance salesman on a Fat Boy Harley Davidson from Kentucky lifts up his shirt for the rednecks. They give him the thumbs down and boo loudly when they see his lily white and hairy chest. A old man cruises by on a raked out Sportster. He has a live goat in a wagon behind the motorcycle. The old redneck couple with missing teeth raise "10" signs like they are judges at the Olympics. They love the goat and have several at home. A sign reads "Long-Term Girlfriend" on the side of the wagon with the goat in it.

An attractive couple rides by with big smiles. They both have a beer in their hands. They wear bathing suits and no shoes on the Harley trike. Their eyes are glazed over after a day of drinking in the hot sun. His shirt reads "My Grass Is Blue."

Dan and Ford spend one night and have a great time eating grilled chicken and drinking some beer. The Artimus Pyle Band was great on the main stage. He was the drummer of Lynyrd Skynyrd until the horrible plane crash in 1977.

They watch a woman in a Brittany Spears school girl outfit ride by on a Harley Davidson Deluxe bike. They get a closer look and notice that she actually resembles Betty Davis about to hit 70 years old. The lady loves to party and ride.

The brothers check out of the cabins and head down the highway to Winchester, Virginia. They are riding to the Candy Hill Campground to camp out again.

Dan had the idea to stay in little cabins at the campground. He thought it would be nice to camp as Wyatt and Billy did in the Easy Rider movie. What he did not know is that the campground has gone downhill since he and Bee stayed there several years ago in their RV.

They ride through a bad neighborhood and pull into the campground on a bumpy gravel road. Weeds and small trees are hanging out into the trail. The campground sign is rusted and cracked.

"Those are some pretty motorcycles. What year are they?" the old man at the front desk asks.

"Thank you. They are 2013 Harley Davidson Breakouts," Ford said.

"I hope they are better quality than mine. I had a 1971 Super Glide and the quality sucked. It leaked oil and broke down all the time," the old man said.

"Yes, the quality improved dramatically when the managers and Willie G. Davidson bought the company from the AMF idiots back in 1984," Ford said.

AMF was a huge company that bought Harley Davidson, ramped up production, ruined the quality control, and then sold it back to actual Harley riders who improved quality tremendously. The bikers pay for the cabins and ride on the gravel trail trying to avoid the potholes and puddles. The park their bikes and head to the shower shack. The cabins have electricity, but no water or sewer.

"Boy, you really know how to pick a nice and clean campground. Are you a little light on dough? Let me know if you need some financial help mister retired soldier," Ford said.

"This place used to be nice when Bee and I came. I promise you that biker. It has gone downhill for sure. I guess the pictures on the web site are a few years old," Dan said.

The bathroom building is falling apart outside and dirty and dimly lit inside. Somebody is always in one of the stalls spreading a foul odor. The plumbing is rusted and leaking. The hot water runs out quickly while they are taking showers.

"Did you pay extra to not have air conditioning? You are such a good planner brother. I do not know how the Army functions without you," Ford said.

"You are very funny. The woman said we had air conditioning. I know she said that when I made the reservation," Dan said.

The bikers dine on mediocre hamburgers and chips and sit around a campfire next to the cabins. They talk about the old days as kids and teenagers chasing girls and riding hogs.

The American flag fuel tank and chrome fenders on Dan's bike shine in the campfire light. The yellow flames and red fuel tank and chrome fenders on Ford's bike glisten in the moonlight. They love to talk trash and gaze at their beautiful motorcycles. "Did you see that Joe's mother died? She was a great cook," Ford said.

"Yes, I spoke with Dennis and he went to the funeral. We had so many good times at his parent's house," Dan said.

"I remember spending the night there one time when I drank too much to ride the hog home. For some reason, I slept in the same bed in the basement with Joe. He was so drunk and in the middle of the night he tried to spoon with me," Ford said.

"That is too much. Did you like it? Did he think you were a girl? I hope he sent you roses," Dan said.

"I guess he was so drunk and dreaming of a girl. He could have had any girl with his good looks, but his shyness prevented that," Ford said.

"I never knew that you and Joe had a different kind of love. How was it?" Dan said.

"You are full of crap. I threw him off and got the heck out of there. I drove home half drunk to avoid the one eyed snake of that Italian stallion," Ford said.

Dan and Ford walk over to the office to get some ice cream. The little store sells many odd camping products and ice cream. The campground owner's son is working. The father is in the corner eating fried chicken with his greasy fingers. His stomach is hanging out between the shirt and belt. There are scars from some kind of surgery a long time ago. He is chasing down the chicken with soup that looks and smells like dish water.

The son looks to be about 40 years old with a dirty t shirt on. His head and eyes are following the every move of a sexy woman in the store browsing. He wants some, but he is not qualified. He does not have good looks or money or anything to offer a good woman.

She has a bikini top on and shorts. She is well endowed and tanned and must be about 30 years old. The long brown hair is shiny and thick. The calves are muscular and perfect. There is no fat on her smooth thighs. She sports summer sandals with fake flowers on top. The poor ice cream vendor can barely take and process the order from Dan and Ford and his mouth is wide open.

"Have you seen anything good tonight? What flavor do you like?" Ford said to the employee. The employee's mouth remains wide open while he stares at the beautiful woman walking around.

"Sorry, I was distracted by Candy. That is not a pork chop. That is US prime mister," the employee said.

"Candy? That is too much. Did you get that pork chop line from the Easy Rider movie? We love that content and painted our hogs like the bikes in the movie," Dan said.

"Yes, I love that flick too. Maybe I will offer her some free ice cream with a scoop of love on top," the weird employee said.

"Good luck. We are in cabins 20 and 21 if you want to drink a beer and see the hogs later," Ford said.

"That was an odd thing for the ice cream man to say. He was obsessed with the young lady," Dan said.

Ford exchanges a smile with Candy in the store. Dan and Ford walk back to the cabins while enjoying the ice cream. One had a cone and the other a bowl. She has the face of an angel and the body of a gymnast.

"Do you think our parent's generation abdicated their parental responsibilities? We ran wild in Florida in the 1970s," Dan said.

"I think you raise a valid point. I bet our parents were determined not to live as their parents did and sought out sex, drugs, and rock and roll. The Hollywood idiots exploited the situation with content about all kinds of immoral activities," Ford said.

"I guess it was an over-reaction to living by the Bible and western Christian values. That is a shame because those values have always made sense to me," Dan said.

"Me too. I was too wild for many years, but always came back to the Bible, God, and Jesus. You took everything too far," Ford said.

"You are too funny. Well, we sure had a great time growing up in Florida and Virginia. Chasing the girls was a blast," Dan said.

"I guess nowadays with so many folks not reading books and articles as we did and continue to do, many people fall for the immorality pushed by the media and Hollywood. They push drugs, alcohol, sex, gambling, pornography, prostitution, gender changes, and worse. The content providers will sell any content to get rich," Ford said.

"I guess freedom is great if you can handle it. I think we must have boundaries. The Bible provides the best boundaries," Dan said.

"This dark beer is delicious. I love anything from the Yuengling Brewery. Have you been on the tour lately in Pottsville? I took a friend from Virginia there a few weeks ago," Ford said.

"They started in 1829 baby in big Pottsville. The old man David Jungling came here from Germany and rocked. His dumb son started a brewery in Richmond, but failed," Dan said.

"I read that he was an arrogant sucker down in Virginia and was sent back home to daddy for money. Nobody liked him," Ford said.

The brothers notice someone walking their way down the gravel campground road. The silhouette finally is revealed in the moonlight. It is a sexy woman with long hair. She must be young and the body is in great shape. She is wearing a bikini top.

"Candy! What is going on? Did you get some ice cream?" Ford said.

"No, I cannot eat too much of that crap. I just needed some detergent to do the laundry. That ice cream just makes me fat in a hurry," Candy said.

"It looks like you do not have any fat on that sculpted body young lady. Would you like a beer? Come take a rest," Ford said.

"That sounds good. We were busy today at work. I work part-time at Staples, but got laid off at a gym due to the Wuhan virus pandemic. The dumb government people shut us down," Candy said.

"Talk to me sister. I bet you are a hard worker. We love business and do not like government at all. How about a hog ride? The weather is so nice," Ford said.

"Are those Harleys? I never rode on one of those. I like the yellow flames. That motorcycle is beautiful. I have a backpack like that," Candy said.

Candy and Ford jump on the hog for a midnight ride. She loves the wind in her face and the loud motor. Ford loves having a beautiful, young woman on the back of his bike. He is lonely after the divorces, but tries to work hard and continue to make tons of money. He loves that fact she complimented his bike and not Dan's bike. That could be a sign.

They ride down a four-lane highway. Ford turns around and tells Candy to look down. He drags the heels of his boots on the pavement. Sparks fly on both sides of the bike. A redneck couple in the car next to them are impressed and stare and wave.

Candy loves the danger and excitement of the hog ride. She never dated a biker before and always just assumed the activity was too dangerous with all the distracted drivers on drugs and alcohol. Ford insists that she wear his helmet for safety.

Ford pulls into a bar for a beer. They get off the bike and talk about the ride. He dogged it so she would squeeze him tighter to hang on. Her small hands around his waist really turned him on. Sometimes he would put his hand on her calf pretending to help keep her safe and stable on the back of the Harley.

"Did you like that? I do not ride at night much anymore, but still love it. I have lost some night vision," Ford said.

"Yes, that was awesome. I never rode on a motorcycle before or dated a biker. How did you generate sparks with your boots?" Candy said.

"That is an old trick from high school. A guy named Mark Williams used to do that and people loved it. I installed heel spurs on the boots and they are metal," Ford said.

"That was so cool. Where are you and Dan going tomorrow?" Candy asks.

"We are heading to New Orleans. I made some cash by selling a classic Corvette and we had to celebrate," Ford said.

"Really? That is too much. I am from there and want to go back soon. I almost bought a bus ticket yesterday, but the prices have gone up. Money is tight during this pandemic," Candy said.

"I will tell you what. You can ride with me if you want to. It is not for everyone, but I can guarantee a great time," Ford said.

"Are you sure? That sounds great. I do not care how I get back down there. I am moving back in with my Uncle Phil until I can get back on my feet. He is the best," Candy said.

A man pulls up on a Honda Gold Wing Deluxe. This is the king of rice burners. He walks so erect that his hips walk in front of his head. His stomach is enormous and his right foot is coming out the side of his worn out slippers.

"Is that a Harley? I bought a Honda for the superior quality and smooth ride," the rider said. He is insulting the Harley brand and thinks all hog riders are dumb. He will probably be beaten if he says this to the wrong biker.

"I bet it is a smooth ride. I love all the plastic. Harley put the quality back into the bikes back in 1984 when real riders bought the company from the idiots at AMF," Ford said. He would not be caught dead on a boring Gold Wing made in Japan.

Ford explains to Candy the history of the Harley Davidson Motor Company and how so many folks think the quality still sucks because it did while AMF owned Harley. Brand new Harleys used to leak oil and break down because production soared without an emphasis on quality at the factory.

"The cup holders and windshield are just too much. If I want that, I will take the car. That guy really needs to read an article about Harley Davidson from the last decade or so. The quality really is unbelievable at this point," Ford said.

They enjoy a couple more beers and then head back to the campground. Dan is fast asleep in his cabin and Ford thinks about waking him up for the big news. He sits by the campfire looking at the beautiful hogs and smiles thinking about this beautiful lady on his hog.

This is a fantasy of a lifetime. He and his brother are on this awesome road trip on bikes and now a sexy, young woman is joining the party. He worries that she is a criminal or horrible person with thugs down the road, but quickly dismisses that negative thought.

Dan wakes up at 0300 in the morning. He hears something scratching and clawing behind the dilapidated cabin. He wonders what it is. Could it be a mouse? Is it a huge sewer rat? He bangs his boots on the floor and it quiets down. "25 or 6 to 4" by Chicago comes on the radio at the next cabin over. Dan loves the long guitar solo by Terry Kath. He wonders if the rat can climb through the hole in the corner of the cabin floor.

Ford is laying on his dirty cot in his dirty cabin and thinking about Candy. What a woman. She is sexy and smart and so young. He thinks back to high school and after when it was so easy to jump from girlfriend to girlfriend. Now it is tough and he gets lonely. He thinks about watching a squirrel walk on a power line from one rooftop to another. The wild animal makes it look so easy. "LA Woman" by the Doors plays on somebody's radio outside their RV.

Dan and Ford love the way the campground is full of life. There are parties and kids running around. It is much more fun than staying at a hotel. It is safer to be outside when thinking about the Wuhan virus also.

Dan lays in bed and thinks about the peanut butter and chocolate brownie he had at the gas station today. They were expensive, but delicious. He regrets not buying a couple more for the road.

Ford lays in the bed and thinks about the Amish guy's sign he saw today. It was huge like a billboard, but shoddy. It said "Whole Real Milk is 97% Fat Free." He has never thought about it that way. What a good marketing message for real cow milk over fake or oat milk or milk made from soybeans. That expensive crap has slightly less fat than the real stuff.

Dan gets out of bed and looks at his hog. He loves the flag paint job and fat chrome wheels and tires. He stares at Ford's bike and loves the flames and how low to the ground the bike is.

Ford thinks about the biker he met today. His teeth were rotten and many were missing. He remembers what Dan told him about the Army dentists. They had a rule in 2003 before Operation Iraqi Freedom where prospective soldiers had to have at least 28 natural teeth. As the war wore on and more Americans did not want to enlist, the Pentagon folks reduced this standard to only 20 teeth.

Dan said that the soldiers had to have at least four front teeth during the Civil War in order to open gunpowder packages. Some idiots pulled their teeth to avoid combat duty. That is the origin of the term 4F, according to Dan.

Ford remembers reading somewhere that you cannot join the US military if you have flat feet or large testicles. You cannot join if you are missing a testicle. What an operation they are running at the Pentagon with these medical standards. "Stairway to Heaven" by Led Zeppelin is playing on the radio.

Dan wakes up at 0800 and walks to the office for some coffee and a Grandma's peanut butter cookie. He walks around in the campground until Ford wakes up at 0840.

"I have a surprise for you," Ford said.

"I do not like surprises. What is it? Your breath is horrible," Dan said.

"I had a great time with Candy last night and she wants to ride with us to New Orleans. She is from there," Ford said.

"Wow! That sounds great. How on Earth did you arrange that? She seems very nice and what a body," Dan said.

"I know. She is hot. I wondered if she had thugs down the road to jump us and rob us, but I can tell that she has a good heart," Ford said.

Dan and Ford sit by the cold campfire and chat for a few minutes. Dan constantly wishes that Ford would find a good woman. They pack up and hit the road. Ford walks over to Candy's RV and she is ready to rock and roll with her backpack. It is red with yellow flames just as she told Ford last night.

"Are you ready to rock? I am so glad that you are going with us. You look divine this morning," Ford said.

"Yes, this is great. I did laundry last night and ready to ride," Candy said.

They see the ice cream man a few doors down carrying a street sign into his RV. It is a construction sign from the highway. The criminal is not hiding his activity at all.

"Does he steal the signs at night? Why would he do that?" Ford said.

"Yes, he is the village idiot. The only reason he holds a job is that his parents own this place. Butch and Gale treat him like a teenager and confiscated his porn collection last week. He is a creep," Candy said.

They ride on the gravel road avoiding all the potholes. Ford dogs the Breakout on the acceleration lane leading to Highway 81. Candy is holding on tight and loving this wild ride. It is so much different than riding in a car. She can tell that the brothers are kind and generous.

They ask good questions and offer everything to her. She really enjoyed the conversation at the campfire last night and at the bar with Ford. The day begins with a bright sun and blue skies.

They are rolling down the highway at 70 mph and loving life.

Dan lets Ford lead and so happy that he has a sexy woman with him. He wishes Bee came and misses his bossy and very sexy wife.

Cars full of parents and kids on vacation pass the bikers. Most of the people in cages stare at the bikes and bikers. Some of them realized that the bikes are painted like the Easy Rider bikes and love it. Some gives the thumbs up. Trucker honk their loud horns.

Ford is so thrilled to have Candy along that he skips listening to his music. He just wants to enjoy feeling Candy behind him and the sound of his huge v-twin engine between his legs.

Dan, Ford, and Candy ride about 60 miles and stop for a break at a diner. The brothers use the restroom and walk around in the parking lot and Candy joins them. Dan walks away to call Bee and chat.

"You two must really be into that biker movie to paint your bikes like that," Candy said.

"You are so right. We have always loved the silly conversations in the movie and of course the Panheads," Ford said.

"Do you think prostitution should be legal? I remember speaking with my mother about that while watching that movie," Candy said.

"Well, that is a tough one. I think I could agree to making it legal, but just not for children under 18," Ford said.

"My mother said the same thing. She was a lady of the night for a long time before she passed away," Candy said.

"Really? That is wild. Did she try other jobs? I guess she tried to discourage that line of work for you," Ford said.

"Yes, she demanded that I go to college and not pursue the flesh trade. I would never do that for a job. She worked at the brothel mentioned in the movie," Candy said.

"Are you joking? That would be amazing. I read that they filmed that scene in a church in the movie," Ford said.

"No, I am serious. We lived near New Orleans growing up and she worked there. She made good money, but got addicted to drugs and alcohol and died young," Candy said.

"That is terrible. God bless you and I hope you got away from that dysfunction at any early age," Ford said.

"Yes, my Uncle took me in when I was young. He is a great man and works hard. I am going to stay in his spare bedroom when we get there until I get my feet on the ground," Candy said.

"Thank God for good family and friends. They are the best," Ford said.

Ford is shocked that Candy's mother was a whore. He is further in shock with her connection with the Easy Rider movie. What a small world this is for sure.

Candy and Ford realized last night that they are both the same in that they both are an open book. They will say anything to anyone and they like that about each other. They shared a brief kiss when he walked her to her RV.

Candy was very surprised that Ford did not try to get her in the bed. All the other men she dated tried to do that on the first date. She was impressed that Ford did not push it and was a perfect gentleman. She is thinking that perhaps an older man is just what the doctor ordered.

"How is Bee? She is hilarious," Ford said.

"Oh, she is doing fine and just working hard with her IT job. She took a video of the geese and ducks going crazy and begging for cracked corn down at the pond. I miss her very much," Dan said.

"You are so sweet, but unfortunately you are so ugly," Ford said.

The three walk inside the diner for some coffee and breakfast. They talk about life and travels.

"Do you rent an RV at that campground?" Dan said.

"I live there, but Butch and his wife Gale will not take any rent. They are so nice and Christian and felt sorry for me after my husband turned out to be gay," Candy said.

"Really? What is going with that? That seems to be an epidemic in the good old USA," Ford said.

"We were married for five years and I thought things were okay. He loved interior design and was very gentle, but I never dreamed he was gay," Candy said.

"Well you can never tell what is going on in somebody's head. You deserve a real man. You deserve a good and Christian man," Dan said.

"Yes and I am not going though that again. There must be a test for that or something. Do you like interior design," Candy asks Ford.

"I have never liked that. I have a 58 year perfect record of heterosexuality. Is that good enough?" Ford said.

They laugh and have a good time eating and talking. She seems too good to be true for Ford. He loves they way she looks, walks, and talks. She loved the way he talks, opens doors for her, and burns money with abandon.

She thinks back to her many boyfriends. Some were very tight with money. Some were rude. Some had violent tempers. Some were cheaters. She has never dated a man such as Ford. She likes this very much and wonders if they can date.

"Did you know that I asked a prostitute in Atlantic City, New Jersey how much she charges? She said the price for intercourse was $50 and only $30 for a blowjob," Ford said.

"Which service did you buy? I know you were a repeat customer," Candy said.

"No, no, I have never been to a prostitute. It is just too much," Ford said.

"I knew that guy named Mike in the Army and he made out with a woman in Germany. They went back to the hotel and she was a he. He was actually a trans prostitute," Dan said.

"That is very nasty. I guess it goes to prove that you should never make out with a stranger," Ford said.

"My mother tried to make it with other jobs, but could not make anywhere near the money. She tried to raise three kids by herself after my drunken father left," Candy said.

"Was your dad a drunk? Ours was too. That is the worst," Ford said.

"He died of cirrhosis of the liver and she died from an overdose. Life can be very cruel. I thank God for my Uncle and God and Jesus Christ," Candy said.

"Amen to that. We believe in God, Jesus, and the Bible for sure. That is the best way to go through this crazy life," Ford said.

"You have paid for everything. Let me pay for breakfast. Butch and Gale gave me $500 the morning we left their campground," Candy said.

"Thank you. You are the money bag now. I guess I should not share with you how much I made on the Corvette in one week," Ford said.

"Boy, you did come out smelling like roses on that transaction mister. You must be living right," Dan said.

"I try to be humble, but with a $60,000 profit it is getting hard to be humble," Ford said.

"Winston Churchill had a good bit about being humble. Someone was telling him how good and humble Gandhi was and Churchill said that he has a lot to be humble about. I always thought that was hilarious," Dan said.

"Did you really make that much dough on a car on Ebay? That is amazing," Candy said.

"I must be extremely smart. This Antifa guy inherited the car from his dead Uncle and just wanted to unload it quickly. I scooped it up with cash baby," Ford said.

The three walk out of the diner to the bikes. They are shining in the sun. They see an enormous woman in a t shirt that reads "Nope" with a drawing of Snoopy on his dog house. The brothers are flossing like mental patients and Candy joins in too.

Dan hits the bathroom one more time. Candy and Ford share a French kiss in the parking lot under a beautiful tree and hug. They are falling for each other and fast. Both of them are full of love and lonely for a great significant other. Fate has thrown them together and they run with it.

Ford never even tried to date a woman 28 years younger than himself. He just assumed that he would be too odd and old for the younger ladies. He is shocked that Candy is really into being with him. She is so beautiful in his eyes and turns him on. He has to fight to suppress his urges and be a gentleman.

Ford and Dan swear that they will never ride hogs without helmets as so many bikers do. They think that is too risky for the head and brain. The morning they left Candy's RV home, he let her wear his helmet. He wanted to ensure that if they went down that she would have some protection for her head and brain.

They stopped down the highway at the next official Harley Davidson shop and bought a custom and huge helmet for her. He has always treated others with immense respect regardless of whether they had money or had none. The Bible taught him this.

Candy scratches and rubs Ford's back while they are rolling down the highway to New Orleans. He remembers that his first wife refused to give him back rubs. What a lady he has found. This is very nice. He thanks God for the good times.

They stop by Natural Bridge on the way through Virginia. Ford takes a picture of Candy with the giant black bear in the massive gift shop. This land with the 215 foot arch was a sacred site for the Monacan Indian tribe back in the 1700s. George Washington came here to see it and Thomas Jefferson actually owned it in 1774.

They walk down the steep steps and by the creek to see the natural wonder. Several employees are dressed up as American Indians and singing and dancing. There is a complete mock Indian village with tee pees.

One actor is talking on a cellphone. His team leader yells at him to get back into character before the children notice and their parents get mad. It is a lovely walk next to the creek and they have a great time chatting.

Dan, Ford, and Candy wait patiently while a group of Asian women take many photographs at the prime photo spot at the waterfall. The women are having a great time laughing and smiling and taking their time to get the perfect pictures to take back home. Their husbands walked back up the trail to smoke cigarettes and to avoid this silly and boring activity.

The bikers mount the motorcycles and ride up the country road back to Highway 81. There is a fake Stonehenge tourist trap on the way. The enormous stones appear to be made of Styrofoam as viewed from the road.

They notice a small zoo with cheap ply-board murals surrounding it. There are many cars in the parking lot with children everywhere. There is even a tiger inside. A man from New York jumps out of his car and urinates on a tree. He has been holding it for a while.

Dan is watching the two lovers on the road and off. He laughs to himself that they are acting like teenagers in love and that is awesome. They certainly have chemistry and he hopes that she is for real and not some serial liar or bad person who will hurt his twin brother. He asks her questions when Ford is not around to verify her goodness and suitability to date his brother.

Dan will not find any bad skeletons in Candy's closet. She was dealt a bad hand with respect to her stupid parents and made the most of it. They made horrible choices and she is determined not to be like them. She worked hard, attended community college, and made her own life. She thanks God that she did not have a kid with the gay ex-husband.

Ford is thinking about that song by Steve Miller where he sings about the woman with black panties and an angel's face. He hopes that Candy is as good as she seems. Ford treats Candy like a princess for the entire trip.

Dan is thinking about how lucky they are to have plenty of success, money, and freedom to live like they do and take a trip like this. He has an idea about getting Bee to join them. He is happy for Ford and his new lady, but it makes him miss his lovely wife more.

Chapter Three
Cruising Around in NC and SC

Candy, Dan, and Ford stop for gas and a walk somewhere near Lake Norman, North Carolina. The traffic is thick because many folks live on the beautiful lake here and commute into Charlotte for work. Candy sees a homemade bumper sticker on an old Chevy truck with a cartoon of Bigfoot on it. The caption above reads "2020 Sucks!" The caption below Sasquatch reads "I'm going drinkin with Daryl." Ford strikes up a conversation with a biker. His shirt has Harley Davidson written on it about twenty times. He loves the brand.

"Hi there. Is there a good place to get a burger around here? We want a break from all this traffic," Ford said.

"You are in luck my man. Easy Eddie's is about five miles down the line. He has great bacon cheeseburgers and hot waitresses," the biker said.

Candy, Dan, and Ford ride over to the biker bar. Several bikers are playing horseshoes and having a great time. They sit down in the outdoor seating area and notice a commotion inside the bar. "Slow Ride" from Foghat is very loud on the speakers.

A young woman is climbing a brass pole attached to the bar. She gets to the top and rings the bell. The crowd goes crazy. Many bikers put money in her tip jar.

"Who owns this place? I have never seen anyone climb a stripper pole and ring a bell like that. That was fantastic. Is there really an Easy Eddie?" Dan asks the server.

"Yes, that is him in the corner cleaning his Panhead. That is his wife over there. Sometimes she climbs the pole too," the server said.

"I always think about my mother when I see people like that. I try not to, but just wonder about her. How could she be a hooker?" Candy said.

"Well I am sure she did some good like everyone else. We are all capable of good and bad. Are you hungry?" Ford said.

Easy Eddie is a grumpy old guy who somehow got a loan and started this successful business. He wears shabby clothes and a long beard. He loves to talk trash and discuss anything to do with Harley Davidsons. He sells parts and repairs used hogs. His wife climbs the pole, rings the bell, and then serves customers.

"Can't You See" by the Marshall Tucker Band comes on the stereo. Ford remembers when he saw them in West Virginia in concert a few years ago at Triple S Harley-Davidson. The singer was flirting with a young sexy woman and her mother in the audience. He told the mother that she could not handle him and that the daughter would be just fine tonight in the tour bus all night long. It was hilarious.

Easy Eddie's Panhead is in the corner of the bar. It is spotless and he rarely rides anymore due to arthritis. It is brown with a custom paint job with a western theme. There are cowboys riding motorcycles and Indians on it. His seat is very thin brown leather with "Easy Eddie" hand stitched on it.

"What do you think about the new Harley electric bike? I think the board and the former CEO were so dumb for trying to push a $30,000 bike on young folks with no dough. It may be the biggest waste of tens of millions of dollars in corporate history," Dan said.

"That is pretty wasteful, but my bet is on the brilliant GM leaders at Cadillac. Do you remember when they put a Cady out that looked like a Chevrolet Cavalier with the cheap steering wheel? They thought nobody would notice. The Cimarron was terrible in the 1980s," Ford said.

"Yes, you raise a strong point my man. The leadership at many corporations is rotten to the core. I guess they get elected or selected and then support each other's stupidity for years and years. The have the dumb gene," Dan said.

"The Cadillac and Harley leaders ruined their reputation for quality for years or perhaps decades doing dumb things like forgetting to focus on quality products. I am voting for you for CEO of Harley Davidson at the next shareholder meeting," Ford said.

"You are full of crap. This burger is really good. You really need to take some ex-lax and get cleaned out," Dan said.

A young couple pulls up in front of the burn pit on a Harley Street Glide. The woman jumps off the bike. She has a huge eagle tattoo above her butt. The crazy biker does a long burn out and then enjoys the applause from the patrons.

Dan walks around in the parking lot looking at the hogs. He calls Bee back in Ashland, Pennsylvania. He misses her very much.

"What? I told you not to call me. I am busy now with work and the pool boy," Bee jokes.

"Hi baby. I know you do not mean it. What are you doing? The lovebirds are still making it. They are so cute getting to know each other. Can you fly down to Asheville and join us for the ride? I miss you," Dan said.

"Of course you miss me. I am lonely too. There is no monkey to entertain me. I will buy a ticket and fly down tomorrow if they have a flight out of Harrisburg," Bee said.

"That is awesome. Get your butt down here. The open road is so beautiful and we are enjoying some delicious meals baby," Dan said.

"Of course you are. You are disgusting. You should only have delicious meals with your wife. See you tomorrow. I love you," Bee said.

"I love you too. Are you in need of daily guidance? I know you do everything your sexy man thinks is right for you," Dan said.

"You are dumb. I need you to do a favor for me since you are having so much fun without me. Get the corona virus and generate some platelets. Come home and donate them to me so I will not get sick," Bee said.

"That is the dumbest idea you have ever had. I had a much better idea. When you come down here, let us buy and put many padlocks on that big bridge over Lake Pontchartrain like the French folks did in 2014 over the Seine River.

That would be romantic to express our love in that way," Dan said.

"That may be the dumbest thing you ever said. Why can't you be smarter? Those French idiots caused the bridge to collapse. They should be put in jail," Bee said.

"You are brutal baby. Why are you so nasty with your very attractive and bright husband? I am strong like a bull," Dan said.

"You are more like a pig. Don't call me. I am watching my murder show and my boyfriend dislikes all the interuptions. Bye," Bee said.

Bee loves any detective show with murders and mystery. Dan jokes that it is unhealthy to watch this content. Her favorite shows come out of the United Kingdom.

Bee is also obsessed with an online show from China. The young woman cooks and eats all the time with her husband filming. Her dog is always lurking and begging for food. She crams large amounts of food into her mouth with chopsticks.

Dan walks back to join Ford and Candy at the table. He shares the good news that Bee will be joining them in Asheville tomorrow. The good times keep on rolling for this group. This is maximum freedom in the awesome and capitalistic United States of America.

The bikers rock on down the highway. A rice burner flies by them doing 100 mph. The brothers take the opportunity to dog their Breakouts and go 90 mph thinking that the police will pull the idiot on the Japanese bike before he pulls them over.

Candy cannot believe that feeling of going so fast on a motorcycle. She has never even been on a minibike or motorcycle. The experience is great fun for her. The brothers take turns speeding up to pass each other and slowing down to let the other pass just for fun.

A guy in a Mustang pulls up next to them and wants to race. They give him the thumbs up, but refuse the dumb offer to race. The guy laughs and points at the Harleys to show great affection and then dogs the Mustang to achieve 120 mph. It is a turbo and he disappears very quickly. His bumper sticker reads "Ass or Gas: Nobody Rides For Free."

Dan and Ford slow back down to 70 mph so they will not get any tickets. They still cannot believe that they get to take this long trip together. They work hard and play hard.

The bikers ride some more and then pull off the highway to stay in another campground in Asheville, North Carolina. They pull into the campground. It is set up like an old western town from the 1800s. There is a huge cigar store Indian on the front porch of the office and general store. They take pictures with the Indian.

"I love those Breakouts with the fat tires. I have a BMW with 300 mm tires on the front and back. What size is your rear tire?" a man asked on the porch.

He is sitting at a picnic table made out of big tree logs. His wife and children are there too. Everyone is enjoying some ice cream. Ice cream goes well with camping. Ice cream goes well with anything.

"Our rear tires are 250 mm and made by Dunlop. It came with a 240, but we think the wider the better. It just feels like we are hugging the road more with that big chunk of rubber," Ford said.

"Very nice. That is my black SUV over there. The Germans can surely make an awesome car. The Americans can make the best motorcycle, the Harley Davidson," the man said.

"Yes, and the Americans sure can make a fine motorcycle. Harley is the best in the world for sure. Is that ice cream good?" Ford said.

"It is the best. My wife and kids love it. I want to buy a Harley soon, but I have to pay off this BMW first. The payments are killing me for the next five years," the man said.

"Hang in there. You should buy a 2018 Harley or newer when you are ready. The new ones are lighter and more powerful," Dan said.

"Dad, why are you so fat? You really need to hit the gym when we return home. Would you like to talk about it? You have really let yourself go," one kid asks his father.

His mother put the kid up for the rude question. Everyone is rolling over laughing with the kid insulting his daddy.

Dan, Ford, and Candy rent two cabins. The campground sits on the side of a hill. They hit the showers after a long day on the rod and head out for a steak dinner. The Outback is not very crowded.

"What kind of dreams do you have?" Candy asks Ford.

"Sometimes I dream that someone is beating me up or I am locked up in prison with horrible men," Ford said.

"That is a dark dream. I like to read books and articles about dreaming and dreams. They are using artificial intelligence to analyze dreams now. I would love to have that job," Candy said.

"One time I had a nightmare that I was married to an old and ugly teacher I had in high school. I woke up in cold sweats. She about 70 years old and I was 40 years old," Ford said.

"Really? You must have some issues with your physical and mental capabilities. I can tell something is not right with you," Candy said.

"I just made that up to see how good you are at analyzing dreams. I am very impressed," Ford said.

"I thought you made that up. I made up my diagnosis too," Candy said.

"Alright you two nuts, let us order up a blooming onion. I have not had that in a long time. If you both eat it, your bad breath will cancel out," Dan said.

The server checks out their bikes. She has a Yamaha 250 and dreams of having enough dough to buy a Harley. She rides every day to college and her job at the Outback.

"I love the paint jobs on your bikes. I saw the Easy Rider movie last year for the first time. My boyfriend said it is a classic and demanded that we watch it together. I will buy a Harley one day after I graduate," the server said.

"Thank you. We love that movie too and decided to paint our bikes like that. I am sure that you will get a Harley sometime. You are going about it the right way in riding a small bike before riding a big hog," Dan said.

"Do you know my mother worked at the brothel in the movie?" Candy said.

"Wow, that is amazing. Did she work in the office or something?" the server asks.

"No, my mother was a lady of the night for a long time before she passed," Candy said.

"I like the way you do not sugarcoat anything. I bet if I do and say something dumb, you will let me know," Ford said.

"I surely will and expect you to do the same mister. Nothing shocks me anymore after growing up like I have," Candy said.

"Our father was a porn star. How about that? He made a lot of dough in that field," Dan said.

"I bet you just made that up. That cannot be true," Candy said.

"You are very perceptive. That would be wild to find out that your father or mother worked in porn," Dan said.

"I cannot believe that so many people buy that stuff. It is a huge business. One girl at my gym told me that she made a ton of money being a call girl and being in pornographic movies," Candy said.

"That is wild. I remember reading about that zumba instructor in Maine who taught zumba and was a prostitute also," Ford said.

"She made a lot of money up there. I think an insurance agent backed her financially. He was kind of like the pimp. What a small business that was," Dan said.

They ride hogs back to the campground at night. The night sky is filled with stars. A long 4×4 piece of wood was lying in the passing lane on the highway. The two brothers barely saw it. They went around it and avoided a catastrophe.

Back at the campground Dan hits the sack early and Ford and Candy sit by the campfire talking into the night. They are really enjoying getting to know each other. It is romantic touching and holding hands and kissing in the Adirondack chairs. They share old stories for hours.

Ford does not push himself on Candy and she is impressed with this older man. They sleep in the same bed, but only hug each other. Neither one wants to move too fast and ruin the relationship. It is romantic for this new couple.

Dan calls Bee from his bed before he drifts off to sleep. They have been married a long time and still very much in love. They harass each other to have fun.

"What? Did you have a fantastic meal without me? I hope you choked on that rib-eye," Bee said.

"Baby you are bad. How did you know that I made love to a rib-eye at the Outback? You must have ESP. We do not have room in our bubble for an assistant husband," Dan said.

"Who said that? I hope you are having fun monkey. I miss you and will see you tomorrow. My flight lands at 9:20 at the Asheville Regional Airport. Don't call me," Bee said.

The next day Dan picks Bee up at the airport and rides back to the campground to meet Ford and Candy. They ride hogs over to the Biltmore Estates for a tour. George Vanderbilt II built the mansion in 1889. It was the largest privately owned residence in America. They take pictures of the motorcycles and each other in front of the water fountain and the 135,280 square foot main residence.

Candy has never been here and is amazed with the property. The others visited here many years ago. They stroll through huge gardens and the big house. Ford is so proud that he can show his new girlfriend this special place. She has never had much money or a boyfriend with money. She has never taken big or expensive trips and loves it.

Dan goes to the bathroom and does not return for a while. Bee walks with him and walks around looking at the furniture from around the world while he is in the bathroom. She stops him cold when he attempts to describe the bathroom experience. Ford and Candy walk around hand in hand. One man thinks they are married and asks them to take a picture. Neither one corrects him on the marriage assumption.

Bee and Dan came here several years ago in their RV and truck. They love to walk in the gardens and up the steep, grassy hill in front of the mansion. They love riding the hog on the Blue Ridge Parkway, but remember when they froze riding back to the campground when the sun went down on a ride long ago. They will ride tomorrow with Ford and Candy. The two couples ride hogs back to the campground. They sit around the campfire and chat in front of their cabins.

"What do you think is overrated?" Bee asks the group.

"If you are talking about anything in this world, I would say children. They are cute like a kitten when they are small and then a pain in the butt like a lion when they grow up. They do dumb things that you told them not to do. It is vexing," Dan said.

"I think older men are overrated. Younger men with fewer wrinkles are much better for the lady," Candy said.

"You are bad baby. Why are you so bad? I need to spank you tonight. I have rugged good looks. Somebody said wrinkles are beautiful," Ford said.

"Who said that? I guess an old, wrinkled, and ugly man said that," Candy said.

"They say the ugliest person in the relationship is always in danger in China. I think that is true. Dan is always in danger now," Bee said.

"I think older men are more attractive than younger men. But that is just me. The wisdom from the wise man just cries out to be worshiped," Dan said.

"I think talking is overrated. Sometimes couples get divorced because they talk too much. There is a time to talk and a time to just be quiet. I like a hardworking man of action," Bee said.

"Those therapists always tell you to talk more in a marriage. I guess that would not be very magical if one spouse has secrets. Some things should remain unspoken," Ford said.

"I will tell you what is overrated. Sports and athletes are overrated. These adult babies are good at a game and that is it. We should cut their pay if they speak about anything, except their sport. They sound so dumb when they get into politics without reading about the policies and history," Dan said.

A man with a bad dye job walks by with a small dog. His hair is bright fake red with natural gray on the sides. "I Love Hogs and Harleys" is on his t-shirt. He owns a Harley Road King and a pet pig. He and his wife are in the RV a couple spots down.

"How are you? We had to get out and stretch our legs. The pig is too noisy tonight," Wallace said.

"Is that your pig? I saw that big thing today. Does he travel and stay with you in the RV?" Ford said.

"Yes, he is very domesticated. He loves to eat sausage and bacon and eggs with us in the mornings. Come by anytime if you are hungry. The old lady loves to cook," Wallace said.

"He looks so huge. How much does he weigh? I see the ramp going into the RV," Bee said.

"He weighs about 300 pounds? He was a baby when we got him from a rancher. Pigs are so sweet and gentle if you raise them right. We live in Roxboro, North Carolina," Wallace said.

"He looks bigger than that. He is very cute and I love the snorting sounds. Ford makes those sounds sometimes," Candy said.

The flag bike and the flames bike are glistening in the campfire. Dan and Ford love to just stare at the bikes. Billy Squier's song "The Stroke" is playing next door.

"We need to find that barbecue place the brothers from home told us about. They said the food is awesome and they are barbecue experts. Maverick and Bear love barbecue, women, and shooting firearms," Dan said.

"I know that is true. Maverick was shooting a Galil assault rifle a couple weeks ago at his firing range on the farm over on Turkey Run Road. That thing is from Israel and is a 50 caliber mean weapon. It is like a rocket launcher. He was nailing a tiny metal target from 3,000 feet with a telescopic sight," Ford said.

The brothers Maverick and Bear made their own firing range. They shoot at targets they bought online that look like Osama bin Laden, the liberal and socialist governor of Pennsylvania, and various Japanese motorcycle badges. Maverick has a bald head and thick sideburns and beard. He looks kind of like Popeye in the cartoons. Bear has a long beard and crazy eyes.

Bear rides a Fat Boy and Maverick a Sportster. They have raucous parties with bonfires and weapons in the woods on their farm. Both of them were in the Navy a long time ago. One time they hired midgets to perform. They wrestled and told dirty jokes. Sometimes 20 hogs will surround the bonfire and firing range on their farm at the parties.

"Have you seen their mother Judy shoot? She is an expert shooter for sure. She has to be 70 years old now. Her hands are still very steady. The whole family should be in the Army Sniper Corps," Dan said.

"Bear had that nurse at the gun range last month. She looks good and they both smoke cigars. She sings karaoke at that pub in Frackville and rides a Sportster," Ford said.

"Have you seen his t-shirt that reads "I Smell a Hippie"? It has a picture of Ronald Reagan asking that question. Maverick and Bear are good patriots and Republicans," Dan said.

"That pig roast they had was great last year. Maverick said that they cooked the pig for 24 hours. It must have weighed 400 pounds. Make sure we get invited this year. They even made delicious soup," Bee said.

Bear and Maverick are the guys to have on your side in a fight. They will destroy any socialists or communists who wander into the neighborhood. The protesters, rioters, and looters in the big cities will regret ever meeting the brothers. Long live the capitalistic and free United States of America.

Dan thinks about how Bee loves food from all around the globe. He thought that was so charming when they met and began dating many years ago. She still gets the biggest thrill going to the international market in Harrisburg for odd food.

"The pig was okay, but I would rather dine on your peeled split mung beans every day. I noticed that a 50-cup serving only has 31 calories and 0 grams of fat. That is great for my waistline. I love that crap from Thailand. I love it sauteed on the oven," Dan said.

"Did you go through my stuff in the pantry? I bet you do not even know what a mung is. We are very smart in Asia," Bee said.

"I know what it is. It comes from the butt of that disgusting mammal in India. No seriously, it is a plant in the legume family first domesticated in India. I love the mung," Dan said.

"The mung bean is much better than your doughnuts and candy. Your waistline is starting to resemble the state line. Your butt is dragging on the floor," Bee said.

"I loved that British rock band Mungo Jerry. Do you remember their hit "In The Summertime" back in 1970? Why was he called Mungo? I wonder if they enjoyed the mung bean," Dan said.

"Is that the screaming rock and roll about sex and drugs? I cannot listen to that loud music. Those people should be in jail. I am going to throw away your CDs," Bee said.

"No baby, you would like this rock and roll classic. He sings about the carefree days of summer. It is free love baby," Dan said.

"I do like the music from Dire Straits. His voice is manly and sexy. Why can't you talk like that?" Bee said.

"I love that band too. Mark Knopfler tells the story being in a pub in Britain with only two other patrons. The band in the corner wraps up their set and announce that they are the sultans of swing. He thought that was so funny because they were not the sultans or kings of anything. He wrote a song about it," Dan said.

"Speaking about your weight, I can get you in for gastric bypass surgery in Pottsville next month if you are interested. Why do you eat so much? It is frightening to be around you eating. Many people could not have the surgery that restricts the size of their stomach due to the lock downs and pandemic," Bee said.

"We were not talking about my weight. I maintain a healthy body weight baby. My BMI is only 30 and I do not need a gastric sleeve. Those large folks have been eating too much ice cream and drinking too much beer while sitting at home doing nothing since March. We need a forced road march every morning to the international grocery store for healthy food kind of like we did in the Army," Dan said.

"I bet your BMI is closer to 50 dear. And you consume ice cream like it is going out of style. That coffee ice cream is terrible. About 260,000 people who eat too much had the surgery last year. I support you baby. Do this for me. I always wanted a sexy husband and never had one," Bee said.

Candy puts another log on the fire. The two couples are sitting in Adirondack chairs and talking trash. Candy, Dan, and Ford are enjoying beer. Bee is enjoying bottled water. A Mennonite couple walk by.

"How are you? It is a beautiful night. Where are you from? I like that hat," Ford said.

"Thank you. We live near Lebanon, Pennsylvania and driving down to Mobile, Alabama to visit family," the man said.

"That sounds fun. My wife and I love the Mennonite restaurant and grocery store near Lebanon. We live in Ashland," Dan said.

"You must be talking about The Creamery. Our cousins own and run that place. They make most of the food from scratch. They are very talented," the woman said.

"Their new building is beautiful. It looks kind of like a log cabin and the outdoor seating area is very nice. Did the Mennonite split from the Amish a while back? I think I remember reading that," Bee said.

"Menno Simons wrote our founding documents in 1536 in the Netherlands. He left the Roman Catholic Church at that time. We are Christians and believe in pacifism," the woman said.

"Are those Harley Davidsons? Our neighbor has one of those. They are beautiful. We have nice horses and buggies to travel around the farmland," the man said.

"Some of our young men have a competition for the best and strongest horse and buggy. They keep them clean as you do with your motorcycles here," the woman said.

"My wife here cleans my bike every week. She is devoted to my hobby. I do not like to get my hands and clothes dirty. She wears a pretty spring dress and high heels while cleaning my hog. She is very sweet," Dan said. He is thinking about the sexy woman washing the car in "Cool Hand Luke."

The Mennonite woman is surprised by this statement and wonders if it is true. The man wonders if Dan really gets his wife to do this chore that seems like it is meant for a man. He would never get his wife to clean his horse and buggy. That is for boys and men only in their culture.

"Do not listen to him. He is joking around. I would never clean that motorcycle. He says dumb things all the time trying to be funny. Do not pay attention to him. Please be normal," Bee said.

The Mennonites walk away hand in hand. They are young and very friendly and open with their conversation. They speak of God, Jesus, and the Bible and try to help others. They work very hard at all they do.

Dan and Ford get biker magazines online and in the mail. They have read the periodicals for decades and love the pictures of the Harleys. Many editions have pictures and cartoons of sexy women washing and just sitting on motorcycles in bikinis or nude. A busty woman washing their hog is an odd fantasy of many superficial and dumb men.

A young woman rides up on a black 2000 Harley-Davidson Sportster. It is totally black with no chrome. She has short spiked hair with sideburns that look like knives. She has many tattoos and very short.

"I like your bikes. My second bike had chrome, but I got burned out on it. I told the dealer before I bought this one that there is to be no chrome on this bike. I love the blacked out look now," the biker said.

"I like that. The Sportster is an American classic. I love that 1200 engine and dual barrel carburetor. You do your own thing and the Sportster is beautiful," Dan said.

The woman parks the bike and walks away to her RV. She has the sort of haircut that requires constant adjustment and trimming. It looks like she shaves it every hour.

"She told me that she is a barber. That makes sense with the detailed haircut. She is really intense about having the motorcycle all black," Bee said.

"She must look at herself in the mirror all day long. Her sideburns and actually all of her hair is so precise. There is no hair out of place on that head," Candy said.

Grand Funk Railroad comes on the speakers. The song is "Bad Time." Dan and Ford used to listen to the band all the time as kids.

"Do you remember that album cover with their heads stuck on body builders? That was hilarious," Ford said.

"Yes, I remember that one well. They must have a great sense of humor. They had on skimpy body builder shorts showing bulges. They had so many great songs," Dan said.

A woman walks by in a tight black outfit. There are three or four straps in the back with meat hanging out everywhere. She wears short shorts and sandals. This is an extra large lady who is not afraid to show a little skin. The breasts are enormous. She is carrying a dozen donuts and three cups of coffee to her RV. She is walking fast in order to plop down in the lounge chairs and consume a few donuts with her man.

"Free Ride" comes on the speakers by Foghat. Dan thinks about seeing them at Virginia Beach during the 1990s. The band had split into two groups and touring at the same time. It was odd to have two Foghats on tour at the same time. They must have had a bad argument.

"Do you remember when we saw them back in the 1970s? They put on a great show in Greensboro. I remember you said that they still rocked years later at Virginia Beach," Ford said.

"I remember you dating that fat girl. What was her name? She had a pretty face and nice hair. You complained about the food budget," Dan said.

"That was not me. There is no evidence to support that. You have me confused with another man. I only dated women in great shape. No pictures survived that period of my life," Ford said.

A young lady walks by walking a dog and carrying a cat. She has animal hair all over her clothes. She is petting the cat. The dog leash is wound around her legs. You can tell that she loves these animals.

"Since You Been Gone" comes on the speakers. Rainbow had the hit during 1979. Dan and Ford remember the song and chat about it and remember the good times and good girls so long ago. Many, many wise girls walked out the door on both of them over the years.

A tall biker with a long beard and his wife pull up on a Road King. His t-shirt reads, "I Work Harder Than An Ugly Stripper." His Harley is black with skeleton hands holding the mirrors. He and his wife look to be around sixty years old.

"How is it going? Have you stayed at this campground before? This is our first time here. I hope they did a deep cleaning. The owners of our last campground had never heard of a deep cleaning. I sure hope we get a safe vaccine soon," Ricky said.

"We are doing fine. This place is pretty nice. This is our second time here. We were just debating whether to take the first vaccine to come along or wait a while," Dan said.

"I will definitely wait a while. My therapist said that this vaccine for the Wuhan virus will slightly alter your DNA. I do not want to grow a long nose or die from an unsafe vaccine," Ricky said.

"I hear you, but I read that it does not alter your DNA. Hundreds of thousands in China and Russia have already taken a vaccine. I guess we will hear about any freaks or deaths coming from those rushed vaccine programs at some point," Ford said.

"Are you into ham radio? I see your sticker on your helmet. I met a guy who told me some things about amateur radio. He was fascinating talking about the signals bouncing off the clouds. Some nut on Highway 78 in PA has one," Dan said.

"Yes, I am on the radio most days when we are at home. Here is a picture of my antenna at the house near Birmingham," Ricky said.

The picture on his cellphone shows a ranch house with a big antenna laying on the front yard. It has four or five metal bars laying across a main section. The antenna looks to be about thirty by thirty feet in size. Rising from his back yard is a bigger antenna with many metal bars. It runs the distance of his entire house and must be fifty feet above the ground.

"We have about two million folks globally involved in the hobby. My radio station bounces sky waves off the Ionosphere that allows me to talk to anyone around the world. It is amazing and fun to speak with strangers like that. That antenna laying in the front yard is my newest toy. I need to erect it when we get back home," Ricky said.

"I bet you get some lonely women on the line. I hope your old lady supervises you and keeps you out of trouble. Those women can be a lot of temptation," Dan said.

"Why do you have to ask dumb questions? Can you not think of an intelligent question for him? This is a complex subject. You get dumber and dumber the more biker events we attend," Bee said.

"The horny housewives are on there all day long. They make many offers, but I walk the line with my sweet wife here. They send pictures sometimes," Ricky said.

"Right Now" by Van Halen comes on the radio at the RV next door. Ricky's wife Jane is very quiet and finally speaks. She is short and cute with long, gray hair.

"Why do you say dumb things like that? I am sure that there are more frisky men on the radio than women. Can you do something useful like go check in?" Jane said.

"Do you talk on the radio? It sounds like fun to speak with strangers from everywhere," Candy asks Jane.

"We play around on the radio together sometimes. There is a nice woman from Columbia I talk to sometimes. We live in Alabama and she lives in Bogota. She and her family grow and export coffee beans for Dunkin Donuts. She complains about the drug cartels, communists, and addicts," Jane said.

"I see that you were airborne. What year did you go through jump school? I went through in 2003. I hurt my back during the sling loader training in week two and barely made it. The jump master kicked a young female soldier out of the plane when she froze at the door. There was no call for that," Dan said.

"Yes, we had a few freeze at the door and then 30 soldiers ran into each other doing the airborne shuffle behind them. I guess just a few trainees are too frightened to jump out of a perfectly good airplane. I visited the lovely Fort Benning in 1994. That was a rough three weeks for sure. Thank God we made it. Motrin and knee braces got me through," Ricky said.

"Amen to that. It took a few weeks for my body to heal from that three weeks at the lovely Fort Benning. Our jump master called us losers all the time to play around. He was great," Dan said.

"He sounds fantastic. My mother sat us down when I was very young and told us to just give up if we tried something too difficult. She advised us to move on to other tasks or jobs we might enjoy and be good at doing. She told us to just give up. Can you believe that? That was the last time we saw her. She left dad the next day for the butcher from the local grocery store. He had a huge tattoo of Popeye on his arm. She was a big drinker you know," Ricky said.

Ricky and Jane walk to the office to check in at the campground. Dan notices the stickers on their helmets. The biggest one is a cartoon of Beelzebub the demon. He has fangs and wings and is shooting a bow and arrow. His muscles are big and he wears a cape without a shirt. His eyes are huge and bulging out of his head. The caption on the sticker says, "Beelzebub Rules."

There are military stickers. One says "Airborne, Anytime, Anywhere." Another one says "Join the Rangers to meet and kill strangers." Another says "Artillery: King of Battle." Another says "Freedom Is Not Free." Another says "Keep America Capitalistic and Free."

Candy and Ford walk around the campground for exercise. They check out the laundromat. It is very clean and nice and has an expensive coffee machine with free coffee. Ford thinks about an article in the Wall Street Journal he read last month about laundromats in Japan. They have twice the laundromats there per capita than in the United States. It is a place to socialize and have fun.

The Japanese have gift shops, cafes, high-speed internet, and chandeliers in their laundromats. The employees must pass a national exam to work there. They like to wash their shoes all the time and visit the beauty salon at the luxury laundromats.

They see an odd entrance to a long, gravel driveway across the street. There is a traffic cone with a plastic owl on top. There is a full-size metal suit of armor with a skeleton head. An old and faded RV is sitting on the dirt. A black telephone with the old radial dial is on the ground. A sign reads "Restricted Area."

"Boy, it looks like they put some time into the lawn decorations. I wonder if they like company or would hate company. Do you see the metal rooster? It must be six feet tall," Candy said.

"I would think they are just playing around with all that stuff. I think the fake fire hydrant is nice. The metal pig would nice for our place," Ford said.

There is a sign that reads "Stay Away!" with a bloody doll head attached to the top. They hear a gun shot. They finally see a heavy set woman with long blonde hair sitting in an old lounge chair in the side yard. She is shooting at paper targets in the back yard and gives them a friendly wave.

"Highway Song" by Blackfoot is playing on the stereo. The music is loud. She is singing and tapping her feet to the classic rock and roll.

There is a wide river next to the road. They see the massive sun reflecting on the water. There are millions of ripples glistening in the sunlight. It is quite a work of art by mother nature. American flags are blowing in the breeze on the telephone poles lining the two-lane country road.

They see a small private cemetery between the road and a corn field. One tombstone has a Harley-Davidson on it. It is sculpted from granite and about five feet wide and four feet high. It reads "Here lies Butch Daniels- This Beloved Biker Loved Hogs and Leg."

Candy and Ford see Bee talking to three young women. Their voices are loud. They are Chinese college students in America. It sounds like they are arguing. They are using Mandarin to communicate. Luxi, Ji, and Shadow are on vacation from Columbia University in New York City. They each have a black pouch hanging down the front of their torso. Big cats are in the pouches looking through the windows.

They are cat people who escaped from NYC because of the virus and stupid criminals. The government folks apparently love the criminals more than the taxpayers up there. The students are taking online classes because the lazy professors canceled in-person class meetings.

"I thought you were arguing. Ford told me that Chinese people always sound like that when they talk," Candy said.

"They are loud for sure. My baby and her family talk like that all the time. You should have heard them in China when we visited a while back. I think it is funny. Bee loves to yell at people in general," Dan said.

"Never Going Back Again" by Fleetwood Mac plays on an RV outdoor sound system. Ford thinks back to the 1970s. He did not have the dough to see them in concert and always regretted not finding some way to see them at their prime.

"What is this movie Easy Rider you speak of? I used to ride a scooter in China and want a Harley-Davidson someday after I graduate if I can afford one. I think the Sportster would be great for me. I worry that they are too heavy for me," Ji said.

"Harley has bikes that weigh from 500 pounds to 900 pounds. You can definitely ride one. We will ride together. Here is my card. That is a classic motorcycle movie from 1969. You should watch it tonight. You will love the beautiful hogs, rock and roll songs, and silly conversation. Just ignore the stupid drug stuff. The Hollywood idiots love that crap," Dan said.

"You can definitely ride a Harley. Our sister, Betsy, is tiny and she has a big twin CVO Breakout. Technically, she is a midget. She rides the heck out of that thing. The key is making sure that your seat is low to the ground. What are you chewing on?" Ford said.

"This is squid and octopus mixed with mung beans. We picked it up at the Asian market today. It is delicious and reminds me of home. Would you like some?" Luxi said.

Shadow is feeding her cat some octopus. He loves it and meows for more. The ladies love their cats. They firmly believe that cats are smarter and more fun than dogs.

"Can I hear the machine run? I heard a Harley-Davidson one time and could not believe how loud it was. My friend's boyfriend has one in College Park, Maryland," Shadow said.

"You should have a chat with your Papa Xi and tell the communist fools to drop the 55% tariff on Harley-Davidsons going into China. America is the land of brave and the free baby! The corrupt commies cannot allow the top symbol of American freedom, power, and success to roam free on the Chinese highways," Ford said.

"You are correct sir. I noticed that the commies over there are really pushing the electric cars because they do not have oil and gas deposits as we have in America. That is their strategic weakness and they fear losing political power. Those electric vehicles are really great for the environment when you consider charging them all the time with coal power plants, throwing away the battery packs every ten years, and all the waste just to manufacture that crap," Dan said.

"The CCP members, families, and friends love the profit rolling in from all the government-owned vehicle businesses and most businesses in China. They do not give a damn about the 90% of the people who do not belong to the communist party. What a mess that socialism or communism is for the normal workers and citizens," Ford said.

"Thank goodness most businesses in the USA are privately owned. We just need to worry about the socialist Democrat politicians collaborating or owning many businesses. They would ruin our great and free America. That is why we must reduce the size and cost of government now," Dan said.

"Alright professors, that is enough of the political science class for today. I just thank God that we live the capitalistic and free United States of America and not under the dumb communists in China," Bee said.

Ford gladly cranks his flames Breakout. He revs the engine over and over for short bursts and lengthy bursts. It shakes the ground with the short exhaust pipes. He motions for Shadow to turn the throttle and she loves it. Even the huge engine's idle rhythm is like music to the ears. But the cats are not enjoying the music and are very frightened. They are so glad that they are in the leather pouches hanging from their owners' shoulders.

"Did I tell you about the park ranger in Florida at the front gate of a state park? He thinks all Asian women are dependent on American men financially. I let him have it and told him that I have a great job and make good money," Bee said.

"I think many older men think like that. They were raised in a different time when men ran everything. I bet he was just joking around. Thank goodness we are equal now," Candy said.

"Bee let that guy have it. He joked that I should watch my credit card around her. He implied that she was a compulsive shopper and I was the bread winner. She got really mad. She is so cute when she gets mad. I think he was just making conversation, but should not say that to anyone. His face was red as he apologized," Dan said.

Chapter Four
Rocking Down the Highway in Georgia

The four riders blow by the Georgia state line. There is huge blue billboard that says "We're Glad Georgia's On Your Mind." A big peach is on the sign too. The peach looks like a huge butt. Perhaps Sir Mixalot lives in the Peach state.

They ride for a while longer and then pull off for lunch. The small restaurant has barbecue. The proprietor also has a small store that sells snacks, used golf balls, very thin t-shirts, and lawn furniture. Many small businesses in small southern villages do not face fierce competition as they do in the big northern cities. They do not have to specialize down here and sell anything.

"Do you see that old man in overalls? He looks just like the guy I used to help in the gym. I worked as a physical trainer in a gym in Winchester for a while," Candy said.

"Really? He is cute with the overalls. I thought about wearing those," Ford said.

"You could not pull it off. He and his wife were 80 years old and the wife could not exercise. He drove to our gym twice a week and gave me chocolate all the time. He said I was too thin," Candy said.

"You are just right baby. You are not too thin. I could look at you all day. I am too fat and Dan will see to it that I remedy that deficiency," Ford said.

"You look fine. I do not want a skinny or weak man. I am not going through that again. We can work out together," Candy said.

Led Zeppelin's "Rock and Roll" comes on the stereo. Ford remembers when the song played during Cadillac commercials back about 2006. He always loved that hard-charging song.

A man walks up wearing shorts with suspenders. His cowboy boots partially cover his very white legs and tiny calves. The outfit does not make sense. He must put it together for looks.

He drives an old Toyota with skulls all over it. There is a skull with pistols coming out of it on the rear bumper. The skulls are stick-on plastic and silver. Single skulls are on the doors and windows. This person must be in love with the skull.

"Those are some pretty bikes. I had a Low Rider many moons ago and loved it. Where are you from? It had a sweet, chrome skull headlight from North Carolina," the old man said.

"Thank you mister. We live in Ashland, Pennsylvania (near Pottsville) and riding to New Orleans. What year was that Low Rider? That is a Harley Davidson classic," Dan said.

"It was a 1979. I had the full skull package on it. It had skull foot pegs, handlebar grips, air cleaner, and sissy bar. I think I read about Pottsville, Pennsylvania in the newspaper last week. A good Republican proposed to name the sewer plant after Joe Biden," the old man said.

"Yes, you are correct. That guy is a good Republican from Shenandoah. He is my good friend James. I think he was half joking, but I am not sure. It was a nice gesture and very fitting for Sleepy Joe," Ford said.

"That would be awesome if they really did that. The symbolism for being full of crap is hilarious. Perhaps I will propose that here," the old man said as he walks away.

"Bee and I play this game by asking about our hopes and fears. I guess we are pretending to be at a marriage counselor or just talking trash. So I will ask you. What is your greatest fear?" Dan said.

"My greatest fear would have to be that Dairy Queen discontinues the Buster Bar. I love that ice cream with chocolate and nuts," Ford said.

"You may be a touch overboard regarding the lust for food my man. Maybe you eat too much. Your stomach is like jelly. That is not very manly," Dan said.

"My greatest fear is that you will always be ugly and lazy. Your face is crooked and the Chinese fortune teller online said that means that you have a bad heart," Bee said.

"You have a tremendous source of wisdom there with the fortune teller. I am sure that she is right all the time. I work hard baby. Let us visit a palm reader this week and get the real truth," Dan said.

"I used to worry that I would become addicted to drugs. I saw many people do that when I was young. Now I fear basements. I have always hated to go down in cold and damp and dark basements," Candy said.

"Wow, I never would have guessed that. My basement is bright with LED lights, warm, dry, and wonderful baby. We can stay down there for days. Sometimes I just sit down there and think," Ford said.

"You are full of crap. I have never seen you think before you speak. This is brutal. Can we change the subject? What is your greatest hope?" Dan said.

"My greatest hope is that you are smart one day and come up with smarter questions. I have been waiting for that for many, many years. You told me that you were smart before we got married," Bee said.

Dan, Ford, and Candy hit the road. An SUV passes them with two kids in the back. The kids are pointing and raising their tiny fists in the air with excitement. They were informed to do that to truckers and they will honk their loud horns.

Dan and Ford dog their bikes and Candy waves to entertain the children. The Harley engines roar to life and the reflection from the chrome blinds the kids. Everyone is having a great time on this trip.

Even the parents in the front seat wave and act crazy to entertain the kids and the bikers. They wonder if these are good bikers or bad. Some bikers are criminals and do not care for non-bikers. The father suddenly starts jerking the steering wheel up and down to the music. The kids go wild and roll down the windows to hear the Harleys and wave.

Candy has never seen anything like this. She wonders if the kids love the Harleys because they look like huge and powerful bicycles. She thinks back to riding bikes on the dirt roads in Louisiana with the other children. She thanks God and Jesus that they were protected somehow from sexual predators on drugs and alcohol.

Her biggest worry was the neighborhood bully. Rachel was tall and obese. She yelled at all the other children and tried to beat up everyone for no reason. She had a voracious appetite and would just grab and consume the other kids' lunches.

One day Candy was walking home from school and saw two kids in the forest. They are lying on the ground and moaning. It was Rachel and the cute guy from her class going all the way. Candy hid and ran away for fear of being beaten for observing the sexual activity. She could have ruined the reputation of the young Romeo for sure for doing it with the fat and ugly girl.

Dan, Ford, and Candy pull off the highway for gas. They are pumping fuel and chatting when a tall and handsome couple pull up on a huge Ultra Glide Classic touring Harley Davidson. Both the man and woman are wearing a lot of jewelry. The bike has a Texas tag on the back fender.

"Hello. How are you? I was ready for a break. How much farther is it? My big ass is sore," the woman said.

"Hey there. I need to take a shit. Can you pump it baby?" the man said. He walks briskly into the big Sheetz gas station to find the toilet.

"We are fine. It is an awesome day for a long ride. You can carry a lot in those saddle bags and back compartment. They are huge. That is very nice," Dan said.

The woman reaches into the back luggage compartment and grabs a pair of her panties and waves them in the air. The couple are having a light hearted argument about her bringing too many clothes on their trip.

"He tells me everyday that I bring too much stuff. If I did not bring these, somebody would not be happy. I wish I still had your waistline sugar," the woman tells everyone while noticing Candy's great shape.

It is kind of like a comedy routine for these fun-loving bikers. The panties look soiled and worn out. They enjoy teasing each other and nothing is a secret. They are wearing matching bracelets made of silver from the north of Spain.

They love sharing too much information with strangers and watching them squirm.

They are tall and wear expensive cowboy boots. Hers are orange and pink and his brown. They look expensive and new. Their rings are huge and sparkle in the sun. She has five earrings in each ear. He has a diamond earring in one ear. He complains about his wife shopping too much.

"I love your custom paint jobs. My step father saw a homemade paint job done with a brush one time on a hog and told the owner that a blind man would be proud of it. I would love spider webs with a green background on mine. That Easy Rider movie was great. I need to see it again," the Texas man said.

"Thank you. Your bike is very nice. Be safe and have a great trip. Do not go clothes shopping too much now. Your wife told us all about it," Dan said.

Candy notices the many small stickers on their helmets that read, "I'm not stupid, but I used to be. I might be impossible, but you sure look easy. If I don't get laid soon, someone will get hurt. Orgasm Donor."

"Keep the rubber on the road. Keep it real. Do not blow it man," the man said as they pulled off on the big touring Harley Davidson. He revs the engine and spins the wide rear tire on the way out of the parking lot.

He was quoting from the end of the Easy Rider movie. Billy enjoyed the ride to New Orleans, but Wyatt thought they blew it for some unexplained reason.

"Now that is a fun loving couple. I bet they are fun to hang with. Don't mess with Texas," Ford said.

A Verizon line worker pulls up and sets up his perimeter. He is repairing a phone line on a telephone pole next to the parking lot. Signs on his truck say "Stay 10 Feet Away."

"Everyone else and the government idiots want 6 feet for virus protection and this knucklehead wants ten. Why is he so special? They should stop maintaining the slow landline phone system anyway," Ford said.

"I agree. Some countries down in Africa were too corrupt and lazy to create a landline phone system so now they are jumping straight into putting up cell phone towers," Dan said.

That reminds me of Cabela's a couple weeks ago. They have new hunting trail cameras that transmit pictures and video to your cell phone. I want one when we get back to Pennsylvania," Ford said.

"We have one of those at our pond and it is great. I love the odd products in that store. This guy was buying refrigerated garlic scented night crawlers and new salted minnows the last time I shopped there," Dan said.

"It is fun to walk around and see all the weird stuff for sale in there. Some man was so excited telling me about finding Canadian big red worms there. He said that they are much better than the American fat juicy red worms," Ford said.

"Did you know that those worms burrow down to six feet in the ground? They can grow to be 14 inches long too. That man really educated me on the fishing bait," Dan said.

"You are a fountain of knowledge. Did I tell you about the security guard arresting the idiot in the wildlife exhibit at Cabela's? I think I forgot to tell you," Ford said.

"No, did that really happen? You did not tell me that one. I would remember that one," Dan said.

"This young guy climbed into the deer area to take some selfies. This security guard took him down with malice. He body slammed the guy and put him in handcuffs. The real police came and took my boy away. I saw his cell phone next to the stuffed beaver," Ford said.

"That is justice. The criminal did not even get to keep his photographs with him in the county jail. That is brutal," Dan said.

"The dude was yelling about his cell phone, but the security guard did not want to hear it. It was the funniest thing I have seen in a while. I think it made the guard's day," Ford said.

"That Dick Cabela, the founder of the store, was one heck of a hunter and lover. He and Mary had nine children over the years. They hunted and watched exotic animals do it together in all kinds of places like Zimbabwe and Ethiopia. What a woman. What a man. They were very sensual," Dan said.

"I bet Bee is a better shot than you. You embarrassed the family at the gun range last month soldier. You could not hit anything. The guy who got arrested for the dumb selfie had a t-shirt that said "Love is Always The Answer," Ford said.

The two couples spend several nights at the Stone Mountain Campground near Atlanta. The massive rock formation has carvings of Jefferson Davis, Robert E. Lee, and Stonewall Jackson on it.

A few protesters stand around outside the gate. They make $10 per hour and are not very motivated. They are disgruntled because the team leader refused their demand for free health insurance. They hold the signs at waist level and refuse to raise the signs above their heads. Most of the time they just rest the signs on the ground. These broke and lazy socialists are very demanding.

The park and campground are beautiful with many trees and a big lake. The four bikers have fun hiking and riding bicycles around the park. They sit around the campfire in the campground at night and talk trash. They ride the tram to the top of the mountain and walk down.

"I loved that laser and the fireworks show was very nice. You cannot get that in the big city," Dan said.

"Yes, although I think I saw a protester on top of the mountain trying to interrupt the show with his flashlight. Perhaps he was just lost and signaling for help," Ford said.

"The view from that cable car was spectacular. I think it was made in Switzerland. Did you see the woman breastfeeding?" Candy said.

"She was not shy. That little boy was thirsty for sure. The men in the car were very interested in the breasts," Bee said.

"It was a wonderful expression of love of a mother for her child. We should see more of that on this trip. Women should feel more comfortable to do that," Dan said.

"Why are you so dumb? Men are pigs. She should at least cover up the nipples. You could see everything," Bee said.

"I wish I had breasts like that. They were perfect and huge. The wives were glancing at her while their husbands had their tongues out," Candy said.

"I never looked at her in order to be respectful. The kid was making a lot of slurping noises on that nipple though. He sounded like a little pig. You could not miss that," Ford said.

"You are full of crap. I saw you looking at her. You sound and look like a little pig yourself. Or maybe an adult pig," Candy said.

"I saw a woman hit her husband on the leg because he was staring at the breast feeding woman. His mouth was wide open," Bee said.

A local couple with two kids strolls by the campfire. The mother is wearing a long dress that is baggy at the bottom and buttoned halfway up her neck. The father is wearing a vest and bow tie and a long sleeve white shirt. They kids are dressed the same.

"They must be re-en-actors at the historic square or tourist trap plantation in the park. Or maybe they just dress like that down here in Georgia," Ford said.

The father urinates behind a big tree and thinks nobody can see him. He is wrong and everyone notices. He is embarrassed as he emerges zipping up his pants. The family looks like it just stepped out of a western town in 1830.

"They do have some buildings here built in the 1790s. I bet they work over there. That boy should not be wearing a Carrie Underwood t-shirt for that job," Candy said.

"Americans used to dress so formally. Now they just let the meat hang out every day and night. The people in France look much better as a whole," Bee said.

The moon is bright on this clear sky night. The Harley-Davidsons sparkle in the moonlight. It is romantic and awesome for Dan and Ford. They view the bikes as their girlfriends. Bee and Candy think they are a little off to worship the motorcycles so much.

"That seafood was awesome. What did you have? The shrimp scampi was divine, but my pants are tight. I feel fat and ugly," Dan said.

"I had the lobster and noodles. Red Lobster is always great. Maybe that is who you are? You are fat, ugly, and dumb. That is who you are dear. Just accept it," Bee said.

"Did I tell you about our grandfather? We called him Poppy and he used to eat the eyeballs of the lobsters. He would pluck the eyes out while my grandmother was boiling them on the stove. He just did it to gross out the grandchildren," Dan said.

"Mama, our sweet grandmother, used to yell at him to get out of the kitchen. He would offer cooking suggestions, which she promptly ignored. She was an excellent cook and loved milkshakes from McDonald's. I would bring them to her when she got old," Ford said.

"She could cook anything. I remember even her chitlins were delicious. They smelled bad while she was cooking them though. She loved to go out for strawberry milkshakes at McDonald's," Dan said.

The next morning they ride hogs over to the 1892 covered bridge in Athens. Dan and Ford take many pictures of the hogs next to and on the bridge. Candy and Bee take pictures of the humans, bridge, and the Oconee River. The sun is out and blue sky bright.

They ride over to the University of Georgia campus for a walk and lunch. Dan tries to ring the Chapel Bell Tower and is rejected. It takes a good tug to ring the huge bell. The others fall down laughing at the weak, weak man trying to ring the bell.

Several muscular male college students walk by in a pack. Each one rings the bell with ease. They ring it to celebrate sports victories, special occasions and just for fun.

"Perhaps you had the wrong technique dear. I need a real man. I need a real farmer or rancher or just a pool boy from college. Is that okay?" Bee said.

"You do have the biceps of a young Swedish girl my brother. This bell tower was built all the way back in 1913. Can you believe that?" Ford said.

Hundreds of college students walk around with books and backpacks. Many wear very little clothing and look so free. Many are eating or drinking while strolling around the beautiful campus.

"Life is good when living on their parents' dime. I guess some of the students are working their way through such as military students. We need to cut the tax money going to the lazy students and help the hard workers," Ford said.

"Can we force all students with government backed loans to perform services like street sweeping and garbage collection for no pay? We should make them join the military to defend this great country," Dan said.

"We should do as the Israelis do. Most citizens over there over the age of 18 must serve in the military for two years. That just sounds right for the awesome United States," Ford said.

Jimi Hendrix's "If 6 Was 9" plays on the stereo. It was in the Easy Rider movie from 1969 and Ford loves it. He has the CD in his truck back home in Ashland.

"Did you know that Jimi Hendrix joined the Army and then regretted it? The judge gave him the choice of the Army or prison for riding in stolen cars. He told his Army commander that he was homosexual and they kicked him out pronto. Don't ask, don't tell baby," Dan said.

"I bet he lied just to get out and get back on the road to fame and fortune. Did you know that he was so dumb that he never even bought a house with all that dough he made?" Ford said.

"He had a one track mind or perhaps two tracks; music and women. I am shocked that he made it through airborne school. That is a rough three weeks we go through at Fort Benning, Georgia," Dan said.

Ford thinks back to his high school days. He borrowed his friend Joe's Kawasaki 250 one day at lunch and rode to the private school his girlfriend, Mary, was attending outside Danville, Virginia. Joe did not know about this borrowing. He did a doughnut outside the classroom window and then stalled the bike.

He could not get it started again and had to push it off the school property before the cops came. He was traumatized by his un-manly performance that day. He could see the entire class laughing at him through the wall of windows.

"They should really blow up the Stonewall Jackson carving on Stone Mountain. He was a jackass when he was teaching at a college in Virginia. He would not allow questions from the students during class. His soldiers probably shot him on the battlefield later on because he was a such a jerk," Dan said.

"They should blow up Lee for letting that idiot Pickett charge up the hill in Gettysburg. He had no chance and killed many of his own soldiers that day," Ford said.

"Did you know that some genius named an Army base for Pickett in Virginia. It is named Fort Pickett. We used to shoot artillery there back in the 1980s. They had the best chow halls there," Dan said.

"I remember that guy cut off his finger at a football recruiting dinner three years ago somewhere on this campus. His kid weighed over 300 pounds and wanted to play for the college," Candy said.

"I remember that too. The daddy's finger flew across the room after he got it caught in a folding chair. I think it was a pinky finger," Ford said.

"A coach grabbed the finger and a cheese stick on the floor. They put it on ice and drove to the hospital, but the surgeons could not reattach it," Candy said.

"That is a shame. I think the fat kid went ahead and played ball here. His father sued the school," Ford said.

"You know a lot about this bizarre story. I guess we can really remember a weird accident like that. Those folding chairs can be trouble. I am surprised the 300 pound son did not destroy a chair and injure himself," Bee said.

"I know. I would not trust Ford in our folding chairs in the barn. He is knowingly over the weight limit of 400 pounds for sure. You can never be too careful about these things," Dan said.

"Did your good brother hurt your feelings? You are not too big baby. I like a real man anyway. Prince and Michael Jackson were too thin. We do not want a skinny, weak man," Candy said.

"You are sweet baby. I see an eagle when I look in the mirror. I could have had a full scholarship for football at any top college back in the day. People said I was very sexy and strong," Ford said.

"You can talk some trash. Do you remember Terry from Danville? He was hilarious when we played golf. He would always refer to himself in the third person as "Daddy," Dan said.

"Daddy hit a good shot! Daddy is going to make an eagle! Daddy looks good today! Daddy had a fat steak last night!" Terry would say back in the day.

Dan, Bee, Ford, and Candy ride hogs though the campus. They ride past fraternity row. There are enormous trees and manicured lawns in the neighborhood. Many drunken young men are sitting in lounge chairs holding up deluxe signs judging the young women who stroll by. Their parents pay the bills while they sit and drink.

Ten of the fun loving kids hold up "10" signs in appreciation of the beautiful flag and flame bikes cruising by. They are spotless and extremely shiny in the sun. The boys hold up their beers in one hand and the Olympic judge signs in the other.

The bikers stop by a hardware store. Ford needs some sunglasses after breaking his old ones by sitting on them. They are in the check out line when an older man begins to yell. He is dressed like Hannibal Lecter in "The Silence of the Lambs." His white t-shirt is very tight, his gray pants are extremely tight and too short, and his face shield cracked and smudgy.

"Back! Get back! The law says we must be six feet away from one another. Get back please! I am going to call 911 on you," the odd man said.

"Sir, there is no law like that. It is all about personal responsibility and personal decision making. Get a grip," the young, female cashier said.

The old man's t-shirt reads "Ted Nugent= Mussolini." He drops his blue and white country dinner plates on the counter and walks briskly out of the store. He is very worried about getting the Wuhan virus. His head swivels around ensuring social distancing.

"Boy, somebody was mean to that guy when he was a child. What is the big deal? Let us just keep our distance and be safe. I bet he ingested some goose dung," the cashier said.

She cranks up the store stereo with "Cat Scratch Fever" by Ted Nugent as she smirks and smiles. Her face is young and smooth with no wrinkles. Her hair is thick, long, and brown. She wears cowboy boots. Her t-shirt reads "Uncle Ted for President."

The loud music appears to push the old man out the automatic doors into the parking lot. He stumbles on the sidewalk and is freaked out. He is a grumpy, old man with wild eyes.

"Do not worry about that old codger. He must have to go to the bathroom. Perhaps he is a little backed up. I think I smelled something. He needs a nappy," Dan said.

"He should stay at home until we get a vaccine. I am quite sure that his current dinner plates will hold up," Candy said.

The young cashier thinks the old guy is an idiot and should not overreact like that. He should just keep to himself if he is so worried about the virus. She is young and strong and enjoys riding horses.

"He reminds me of my father. Nobody deserves a person like that. What a pain in the butt that would be. Most men in China think they are better and more important than women," Bee said.

"Did you hear about that construction worker in Massachusetts who ate black licorice for a few weeks and died? He was 54 and consumed a bag and a half every day then keeled over. What a man!" Ford said.

"I wonder why he ate so much of that crap. I could not finish one piece right now. Maybe he was on some special and really stupid diet," Candy said.

"I think Oprah eats that stuff to maintain a healthy body weight. Her BMI is down to 50 this month. That is what Peoples magazine reported," Dan said.

A young couple from Japan pull up on a 2020 Harley Davidson Fat Boy with the 114 CI engine. It is blacked out with fat tires. The couple is short and flew in for the bike rally in Panama City Beach. They rented this bike in Jackson, Mississippi for the ride to Florida. They wear masks most of the time to protect from the virus going around.

"Hello there! I like that bike all blacked out. That headlamp is huge. Does the wind blow you at all with the solid wheels?" Ford said.

"Good day. Thanks, and the wind does not blow us at all. We rented this one and had to leave our Panhead at home. I usually only ride stripped down hogs, but this Fat Boy is fun," the Japanese rider said.

"Do you like to ride? My husband rides much more than I do, but it is fun," Bee said.

"I do like it. My husband goes too fast sometimes, but we have fun. This bike is a lot smoother than our hard tail at home. We love the wide open spaces in America on a bike. Japan is crowded in most places," the wife said.

"Japan is Harley's third largest export market. I remember reading that Harleys were made in Japan before WWII. That is amazing to think about just before all the killing in the war," Dan said.

"Yes, many people in my country love Harleys for the look and sound and also love the Japanese bikes for speed. Most bikers there ride the bikes made in Japan of course. The price is much lower than the Harley Davidson," the husband said.

The husband is short and wears white cargo pants tucked inside his tall brown boots. There is Japanese writing on the right pant leg and a patch that depicts a bottle of sake (rice wine). He wears a black shirt with Harley logos all over it. He has a couple tattoos and thick black hair.

The wife is very short and dressed in black leather pants with a pink and white top with a Japanese flag on the upper sleeve. Her hair is long, black, and thick. You can tell by speaking with them that they are anti-government and love freedom.

"Do you wear the mask often at home? I read that it is more normal over there than in America," Bee said.

"Yes, many citizens wear a mask in our country. Many places are crowded and people protect themselves from disease that way. Most of our land is mountainous and rough with only 12% arable or suitable for farming," the husband said.

"Some people here freak out and almost refuse to wear the mask. It is funny to watch. I saw this one man in shorts and flip flops tell the cops that they would have to tase him before he would put on a mask. The police just arrested him," Candy said.

"They should have lowered the bike for you. I noticed you must stretch your legs to reach the road when you stop. You are on the tiptoes. You two look fabulous on that bike though," Ford said.

"Yes, my seat height is only 20 inches on my Panhead, but this seat is much higher. But we can make it work. Harley Davidson all the way," the husband said.

"Do you have expensive toilets over there? I read about gold ones, self cleaning toilets, toilets surrounded by aquariums, and toilets with ski slope murals all around them. Americans will only pay $200 for a toilet while Japanese are paying $10,000 for the stool," Dan said.

"Yes, that is true. We have an electric toilet encrusted with fake diamonds all over it. The cost was $5,000 USD and it has many LED lights. It is shiny, self-cleaning, and beautiful. This is common in our nation," the wife said.

"My parents have an electric dual tornado flush toilet. It is cotton white with adjustable height. The UV light kills all bacteria, virus, and germs. It cost them $14,000 and worth every penny. It has an automatic lid and flush system. We will upgrade later when the money is not tight," the husband said.

"I am going to buy one of those when we get back to Pennsylvania. I am tired of the cheap toilets. I deserve the best. I will have to run power in the wall over to the bowel movement area first. That will be awesome," Ford said.

"Somebody really needs to tell the folks in the Middle East about nice toilets. They still defecate in holes in the floor. And it was hard to find toilet paper in Kuwait back in 2003 during the war. They use their hands and a water hose to wipe and think we are wasteful with all the paper. They are are very nasty," Dan said.

"Ain't Talkin' Bout Love" by Van Halen plays on the store stereo. The bikers love the rock and roll music everywhere. The cashier is almost dancing while checking out the customers.

"They need to have a toilet world exposition in Kuwait. It should be modeled on the world's fair in the old days to teach the Kuwaitis about cleanliness and spotless bathrooms and toilets. Only the finest toilets from around the world may be displayed. Believe me, they can afford the toilets with the free checks from the Kuwaiti Oil Company every month," Ford said.

The Japanese couple zooms off on their rental bike. The wife's long hair is flying behind them. This is a vacation of a lifetime for this young couple. They will hang out with a small Japanese biker club at the rally and enjoy watching all the wild and crazy American bikers.

A tall and skinny man walks up to chat. His gray chest hair is hanging out from his v-neck white t-shirt. He wears tight parachute pants tucked into his cowboy boots. His skin is white as a sheet.

"I'm just trying to get my thing together man," the stranger said. He sees Dan and Ford's bikes and realizes they painted them just like the bikes in the classic Easy Rider movie. He speaks in a calm and low voice as Wyatt did in the movie for comedic effect.

"I like that. You must be a fan of that movie. Is that your Sturgis over there? I bet that is from 1979. I loved that Low Rider-type hog. I had a 1979 Super Glide," Ford said.

"You are close my man. It is a 1980 Sturgis. I bought it brand new and have not changed anything. It just really struck a cord with me. My old lady thought it was ugly with the orange wheels and derby cover. I love your bikes. Have a blessed day now and keep the sunny side up," the stranger said.

The stranger walks away. His pants are too tight and look very old. His old lady is short and obese. She is very bossy and wears short shorts and a halter top with meat hanging out on all sides.

"I love that bike with the kick start. I want to see him kick start it as we used to do. It looks brand new. I miss my 1979 Super Glide. That was my baby. His old lady looks like your girlfriend in 10th grade," Dan said.

"It is wild to think that we kept our hogs inside the motel rooms at the bike rallies in Myrtle Beach and other places. Do you remember that? We were afraid of criminals stealing our chrome or entire hogs. We had to step around the hogs to go to the bathroom in those tiny motel rooms. They never complained that we left oil stains on the carpet," Ford said.

"Look at you! You are all dried out and ugly and fat. I am quite sure that your girlfriends did not look good at all. You are lucky to have me. How many girlfriends did you have?" Bee said.

"No, no, there is no evidence of that. I am so glad that we did not have digital cameras, cellphones, or the internet back then to document all our mistakes. All of your girlfriends did not exactly look like Melania Trump my man," Ford said.

"Wouldn't it be funny if one of your old high school girlfriends surfaces and posts pictures of you online? That would be the ticket. I would love to see that. Perhaps she is still interested in you," Candy said.

"We only dated nice girls. They were all prom queens with stellar reputations. One of them had plans to become a doctor. We had only US prime and no pork chops," Dan said.

"Yes, our high school girlfriends all attended church and did volunteer work with senior citizens. They were so sweet and innocent. They had to be in by ten at night," Ford said.

"I bet they were very experienced. You should be ashamed. You are a bad person. I deserve better. Is that pool boy still available? Let us hire him when we return to Ashland. I joined Adam Scott's fan club. Perhaps we can meet soon for a meet and greet. He is beautiful," Bee said.

"I cannot argue with you baby. Adam was immaculate on the 18th green at Augusta in 2013 when he won the Masters. I cannot compete with that. Perhaps I will join the fan club too. But there will be no touching at the meet and greet. You cannot get the pool boy without the pool," Dan said.

"Okay, let us build a swimming pool. You know Adam is only 40 years old. Those cougars seem to have a great life. What about that? How old are you now?" Am I too young for you now?" Bee said.

"No, no baby. Perhaps we should have worked harder. We could have fame and fortune too like Adam. How about that? It hurts deep down inside to realize that he is younger, sexier, and much more successful than your husband. I can get some work done on my face and turkey neck," Dan said.

"You should have worked harder. I work harder than you. I wonder what Adam likes to do in his spare time. Perhaps I will write a letter as a super fan," Bee said.

"I am comfortable with the fact that I never got invited to Augusta. I will never own the coveted green jacket. I cannot drive down Magnolia lane. I will never spend the night in the crow's nest. I have to live with that shame all my life," Dan said.

"I am glad that you are comfortable with your lowly situation. But do not hold me back from being with the man with the green jacket and glory. I deserve the best," Bee said.

"You are so sweet. Don't ever change. Perhaps we can see Bubba Watson or Dustin Johnson slip on the green jacket in November and cry like a baby. That would be so sweet to cap off the year of the pandemic," Dan said.

A young woman walks by in an expensive sun dress with a Gucci bag. She has makeup caked on her face. She even has makeup caked on her cleavage to make it appear larger and deeper. The eye lashes are huge.

"Boy, she is single-handedly keeping the beauty industry above water. I read that women are buying much less lipstick, blush, makeup, and nail polish because they are stuck at home during the pandemic," Dan said.

She wears a thick 20 inch 18kt gold fine Byzantine necklace made in Italy. It shines and glows in the sunlight and has the coveted lobster clasp. It is highly polished and looks brand new.

"I saw it advertised in the Wall Street Journal for $4,000 a few weeks ago. It is beautiful and made in Italy. If Dan had worked harder, I would be wearing one right now. I bet Adam's wife has several like that," Bee said.

"I could smell her perfume from a mile away. She looks very clean and spotless and would be very much in place at the Masters. I wonder what she looks like under all that stuff. How long does it take her to get ready in the mornings? I dated a girl in high school like that," Ford said.

"I bet you dated some winners. I think I will join the Adam Scott fan club and get a younger man with Bee. That just sounds right. We can compare notes. Maybe Adam has a hot younger brother from Australia. Fewer wrinkles beats many wrinkles on a man," Candy said.

"Pride and Joy" by Stevie Ray Vaughn comes on the speakers. Dan and Ford are playing air guitar on this one.

Chapter Five
Rumbling Through Alabama and Mississippi

Candy, Ford, Bee, and Dan are enjoying a barbecue lunch at the diner. They talk about the wild drivers on the interstate. They mention things that they saw and wonder if the others saw them too.

"Did you see that nut in the red truck trying to back up to the deceleration lane because he missed the exit? He is one brick short of a load. That is what rednecks say," Dan said.

"That is what you say. You would fit right in with the redneck group. You would be welcomed into the dumb group," Bee said.

"I am so glad that you amuse yourself. That idiot is going to cause an accident because he will not drive to the next exit and turn around," Dan said.

"We Are The Champions, We Will Rock You" by Queen is playing on the store sound system.

Dan, Candy, and Ford sing along and enjoy the barbecue. Bee tolerates the rock music, but prefers softer songs such as "One More Night" by Phil Collins.

Bee consumes more barbecue than Dan, Ford, or Candy and she is the smallest person at the table. This petite Asian woman loves the food, but walks at least ten miles per day. She jump ropes on some days too.

"Did you see that dead deer? It looked like someone hit it and then cut off the antlers. That thing was huge," Candy said.

"That is what you call an urban hunter. I wonder if they mount the antlers on the wall and tell people that they shot it while out hunting," Ford said.

They are sitting outside to avoid the virus when an odd guy pulls up on a moped. His shirt is red and "North Pole Celebrity" is printed in front of a white star. His pants are blue with tiny snowmen in wizard hats printed all over them. He blares the song "More Than A Feeling" from Boston on his tiny radio attached to the handlebars with some twine.

"Boy, I love your motorcycles. I would die for one of those. Did you hear the new song from the Rolling Stones archives? It sucks. They just played it on the radio," the middle aged man said.

"I have not heard anything new from them in decades. I guess many of their songs sucked," Dan said.

The moped rider looks as though he just got out of bed in his night suit. He is so hyper and happy. His bedroom slippers are worn out. He smokes a cigar.

Dan's bike with the American flag on the tank is extremely bright in the sun. The red, white, and blue paint is very bright. Ford's bike with the yellow flames on the red background gets everyone's attention with the clear coat. The paint looks wet, but it is dry.

"I get my coffee on the outside. I had a Keurig, but it quit. My mom bought it for me. I love the breakfast blend here, but hate to wear this mask. You must have plenty of money. If I had your money, I would burn mine," the man said.

"We need a vaccine. Is that bike hard to learn on? It looks like fun for a summer day. I want to learn to ride," Candy said.

"No, my sister gave it to me and taught me how to ride it. She bought a Harley Low Rider. It is beautiful with red and blue paint," the man said.

"I can teach you how to ride baby. I have so much love to give. Would you like some?" Ford said.

"I love your weird comments baby. Okay, that sounds great. I guess you are qualified after decades of riding. But you seem unstable. I need a stable person," Candy said.

Candy and Ford love to rib each other. Bee and Dan are amused to watch because they have the same dynamic. Bee is the queen of the toxic comment and notices everything.

"Why do you eat so much? It must be some deep psychological issue. We do not need to buy a pig because we already have one. You are a real man," Bee said.

"Leave me alone. I love to eat anything. It is the only thing that makes me happy. This barbecue is good, but they should serve it warmer. I better take it easy or my butt will be dragging on the floor," Dan said.

"Your butt is already dragging on the floor. It is very disappointing. You have an elephant butt. Did you see the elephants in the circus? That is exactly what your buttocks look like," Bee said.

"You know that guy's sleep wear looks like yours. I love yours with the monkey eating a banana all over it. I think it is a pink one piece with enclosed feet. You look like a child in that thing, very cute," Dan said.

"You bought that silly sleep wear in Atlantic City when it turned cold last year during our trip over there. It is soft and warm and very nice," Bee said.

"I remember that trip. I had that awesome shrimp dinner out on the enclosed pier. That was delicious. I love that pier with the sand and Adirondack chairs," Dan said.

"You always remember the food. Why is that? The light and water show was pretty out at the end of the pier," Bee said.

"I have always wanted to go there. My parents talked about gambling and having a great time up there, but I have never been," Candy said.

"I will take you there anytime you sexy thing. We can take the truck for comfort. I do not want to ride the hog in all that traffic with the reckless drivers in New Jersey. You are my queen baby," Ford said.

"I guess you are too old for that. Is that right? Are you too old for me? I need a younger man. Bee makes a convincing argument," Candy said.

"Your younger man will have horrible credit and bring you down baby. I can lift you up with my Experian score of 820," Ford said.

"I thought you were at 840. I slipped down to 795 last week and still sad about it," Dan said.

"I took a hit for some unknown reason. Dan and I have a contest regarding credit scores. It has been simmering since college," Ford said.

"I do not even know my credit score now. I think it was 730 two years ago when I applied for a loan. I find your belief system fascinating. What that in a Seinfeld?" Candy said.

Candy has heard Bee, Dan, and Ford quote from the Seinfeld show many times. She watched some episodes and remembers some of the lines too. The silly conversations reminds her of the ones in the Easy Rider movie. Meaningless conversations about minutia or trivial matters can be hilarious.

"Do not do that in public. The server saw you," Bee whispers to Dan.

He has the bad habit of rearranging his stuff after he sits down. He reaches into the pants and turns them over. He thinks nobody notices, but sometimes they do. Bee is trying to get him to not act like a caveman.

"I know baby, sorry. I have a medical problem of too many veins in the testicles. I am a victim. My balls are huge," Dan said.

"Please be normal. That is very odd behavior. You are not a wild animal or caveman. People think it is gross. I need a younger man," Bee said.

"Hey, three is a crowd. You do not want that baby, trust me. You only need one good man," Dan said.

"Who said that? Our goose seems to like having two boyfriends. Adam Scott looks divine on the PGA tour. You know that he is only 40 years old. How old are you?" Bee said.

"That is cold baby. I am a youthful 58 years old and strong as a bull. I can swing baby with the best of them," Dan said.

"Tell me about it. I need a young man. They have so much capability," Bee said.

"I think Bee raises a valid point my man. You are way past your prime by brother. Very nasty indeed," Ford said.

"Look at you big boy. You remind of a water buffalo at one of those dried up ponds in Africa. Somehow they find the nutrients and get big and fat eating something over there," Dan said.

"You folks do not hold back. I love it and just need to stay out of these toxic conversations. All I say is that I would love to have Bee's body. You must work out all the time," Candy said.

"Thank you.. I walk a lot on the farm and run on the stair master. Dan and I do walk all the time and ride bikes. I want to take up boxing as the women do in those dumb drug commercials on TV," Bee said.

"Did I tell you about the boxers while I was at Fort Jackson for basic training? That was a good one," Dan said.

"No, I do not think I have heard that one. Did you box while you enjoyed basic training in South Carolina? I cannot watch boxing anymore. It is just too violent," Ford said.

"No, I did not box, but our battalions had boxing champs and they competed with other battalion champs. The winner was the brigade champion and he got to go to California for the top championship. Our boxer was short with small muscles and a couple Harry Potter tattoos. The other boxer comes out into the ring and he is tall and very muscular with blond hair," Dan said.

"He sounds like an Aryan from the Hitler army. Did he wipe the floor with your puny guy?" Ford said.

"No, that was the funny thing. Our guy hits the massive guy in the head in the first five seconds of the match and the giant goes down. Everyone there went crazy. He just lays on the mat and cannot get back up. It was so funny that the giant had a head of glass. That was in 1984," Dan said.

Two guys pull up on a Road King and Street Glide. They have images of rebel flags, Robert E. Lee, Jefferson Davis, and confederate soldiers all over their gas tanks and fenders. The bikes have Tennessee tags.

"Boy, those guys better not run into the BLM folks. There could be trouble. I wonder where they are heading," Ford said.

"They are really into the south. Perhaps they love the southern United States and not the slavery crap," Dan said.

"I saw a documentary about Lynryd Skynryd the other night. Ronnie Van Zant loved the south, but was not racist. He wrote Sweet Home Alabama about that," Ford said.

"I love that song. What a classic that is for sure from Jacksonville, Florida. Only about 10% of the southern people had slaves in 1860. I love that song "That Smell" by that band," Dan said.

"Can you be my slave? I always wanted one and never had the chance," Candy said.

"I would love to be your slave baby. You are very bad. I like it. You can spank me anytime," Ford said.

"I just want to boss you around. I did not ask you if you are into sadism or masochism. Perhaps I am seeing your bad side now. Can you please just stay on your good side?" Candy said.

"I did not know that I had a good and bad side. I definitely have an attractive side and an ugly side," Ford said.

"That is only partly correct brother. I only know your ugly or fat side. It just smothers and overshadows the attractive and thin side. You look like a tick," Dan said.

A bald man walks through the parking lot wearing headphones. He uses two metal walking sticks as though he were hiking on the Appalachian Trail. He looks to be about 60 years old and wears a wrinkled and loose fitting silver weight-loss outfit.

The bikers have seen this thing advertised on TV late at night. The top and bottom is made of thick plastic-type material that makes you sweat in order to lose weight. It can be dangerous on hot and humid days. His sneakers are bright baby blue in color.

"I am going to buy you that outfit chubs. You could drop a dress size in a week," Dan said.

"No, no, I am working on a system. I bet that guy is sweating like a pig. I wonder if Harley makes a suit like that," Ford said.

"He looks like an extra in a low budget science fiction movie. Remember "The Blob?" The characters from other planets are always wearing the plain and silver outfit," Candy said.

"I wonder if it really works. Perhaps he just sweats a lot and then goes back home and eats too much. I can see that happening. I bet it is made in China," Bee said.

"I feel like I am at the peak of my manliness. Well, to be honest I am way past the peak of being manly. I had it for a long time and then lost it," Dan said.

"I would like to find a man at his peak of manliness. That would be very nice. Talking is overrated," Bee said.

"Baby, we need to talk more. I must be twenty years past the peak of my manliness and attractiveness. Our conversation is more important than our physical chemistry right baby?" Dan said.

"I do not need that at this point in my life. Can we get some help with a man at his peak or slightly before his peak of manliness and attractiveness? There is no need for talking now," Bee said.

"I do not remember you ever peaking in being manly or being attractive my brother. I always looked much better than you," Ford said.

"I wonder what age is the peak for a man? I guess it would be in his twenties. You two are a long way from that," Candy said.

"No, no, it may seem like that to the untrained eye. We are still going up for you ladies. Somebody wrote that we peak at age 60," Dan said.

"Who said that? I bet an old man said that crap. You must be thirty years past peak darling. We need help. Three is not a crowd as they say. We need to expand our bubble," Bee said.

The four bikers spend a few nights at a campground in Biloxi, Mississippi. The campground is wide open with gravel and no trees. It is one block from the beautiful beach and ocean. There are still many vacant lots and destroyed buildings and houses from Hurricane Katrina in 2005. The storm surge exceeded 12 feet above the ground level.

The two couples stay in two cabins next to an old RV. They see the shadow of the occupant, but never see the actual occupant. It looks like the RV has not been moved in twenty years. This is their permanent dwelling with several cats roaming about.

Bee, Dan, Candy, and Ford spend the days riding hogs next to the ocean, dining on great seafood, and walking on the boardwalks. Many buildings have high water marks denoting how high the ocean came in many years ago. They stop for ice cream.

They see a crazy biker with very high ape hangers pull up on a Harley Davidson Low Rider. He has a butt wrap on his helmet. It is flesh color and looks just like a human butt. It wraps around his entire helmet with the crack on the backside. There is a huge Van Halen tattoo on his arm. "And The Cradle Will Rock" is playing on the bike's stereo.

His hog is the color of flesh also. Dan and Ford have seen a lot of hogs, but never one this color. They walk over to chat with the odd biker. He has a thick and huge wallet on a chain hanging down his pant leg.

"Hello. You must like the ladies. Are you a pimp? I love that hog with the flesh color. We have never seen one like that," Dan said.

"Well, thank you. My old lady and I are charter members of Saggy's nudist colony near Tampa. I thought it would be funny to paint my bike to reflect that awesome experience. The members love it," the odd biker said.

"That is awesome. Do the ladies look good at your nudist colony. I would think most of the nudists do not look too good," Ford said.

"Most of the members look pretty good. There are some big ones though. The big ones love to watch the sexy ones. But the large members get plenty of action if they want it. Do you have a smoke? I quit buying cigarettes, but I did not quit smoking," the nudist said.

"Sorry, but none of us smoke. There is a WaWa down that road. It just opened up and only for moochers," Dan said.

"That guy told me that he is a retired psychologist. That sounds about right. He is part of the problem with the unproven theories and unproven prescription drugs infecting folks," Ford said.

"Really? He is just like those nuts who set up and ran the Stanford prison experiments back in the 1970s. They taught the fake lessons from these experiments to generations of psychology students. They lied about the "sadistic" people role playing as "guards" toward the fake prisoners. They told the guards to behave that way and be mean to the fake prisoners," Dan said.

"Those same dumb psychology graduates are the same people giving drugs out like candy today. That is a shame for everyone," Ford said.

"You really should be in prison. And not a fake prison. You should be in the prison within a prison or solitary confinement my man. I could pay for your cigarettes and candy once a month as a treat. You could get some humorous prison house tattoos and big muscles to help ease your re-entry into society," Dan said.

"My last old lady let me know that she needed some space. That phrase in the nudist colony is code for "she wants another dude." That hurt me for a while, but I found a sexier old lady. Everything will work out fine now. Have a wonderful day," the nudist said as he walks away.

They tour Beauvoir, the Jefferson Davis Home and Presidential Library. James Brown (not the awesome singer) built the house in 1852. Sarah Dorsey bought the house and named it Beauvoir signifying its beautiful views of the beach and ocean.

Sarah just happened to be friends with Jeff Davis's second wife. She rented a cottage to him in 1877 after the war and then he bought the estate in 1879. The bikers are walking around in the museum when one of them spots a dress in a glass case.

"What is that? It sure is a fancy dress. This house is awesome. The ocean breeze just flows right through it. The house designer ensured that," Bee said.

"Jeff Davis wore this dress while he was escaping from the Union soldiers during the civil war. He wanted them to think he was a woman," Dan said.

"Oh, this sign says that the northern newspapers ran pictures and stories about that. They said he was a coward and representative of all the bad folks in the south," Bee said.

"I guess old Jeff was secure in his masculinity to sport the dress. I wonder if the southern soldiers made fun of him too," Ford said.

"They locked his butt up at Fort Monroe in Virginia. I toured that place several years ago when I pulled Army duty at the Norfolk Naval Station. He was there from 1865 until 1867. The Pope wrote him a nice letter. That was a nice gesture. A seagull dropped a bomb on my head one day over there. That was very nasty," Dan said.

"That ice cream looked good in the snack bar. Let us adjourn to have some and discuss and debate the historical record. I have to expeditiously walk to the bathroom, excuse me. Something did not sit right," Ford said.

"I thought you just ate. You are like a wild animal or something. Beavers eat all the time like you. Did you see Jeff's wife? She was wild looking," Candy said.

Ford walks briskly to the outhouse to do his business. He realizes there is no toilet paper after it is too late to terminate the proceedings. He uses his shirt to clean his back side and walks to meet the others shirtless. They are laughing at the site of him with no shirt on at the tourist trap.

"Wow, you look much better in full winter clothing brother. That chest and stomach are very nasty. I am traumatized. You look like that fat singer Meatloaf," Dan said.

"Very funny. Will you please just go and buy an overpriced Jefferson Davis t-shirt in the gift store? I did not check the toilet paper roll first," Ford said.

"You should just ride home shirtless. You could set an odd trend for older, ugly bikers," Candy said.

"Do not listen to Dan. He looks like a tick when he takes off his shirt. He has really let himself go. It is sad to watch. He likes comfort food a little too much," Bee said.

Dan gives the tour guide a $50 tip. The older woman is moved to tears and hugs him. Money is tight and she had her hours cut during the pandemic. She is dressed in a period outfit from 1865 and the tip puts a pep in her step.

"Here Comes My Girl" by Tom Petty comes on the speakers. The young employees at the Jeff Davis house are jamming to the rock and roll.

The old woman in the period outfit dances and sings along also. The hogs look beautiful in the sunlight on the sand with the old mansion in the background.

Ford watches closely as Candy walks ahead of him. The physical attraction is very powerful. He cannot keep his eyes off her very toned legs and muscular calves. He loves her thick and long hair too. They are kind of like two bees with Candy releasing sex pheromones that attract Ford. He cannot resist her.

The tips keep getting bigger on this ride from Pennsylvania to Louisiana. The brothers are playing a game of who can leave the biggest tip for the hard workers. It has been several years since Dan and Ford realized that they do not need to work anymore unless they want to. They have earned pensions, IRAs, 401Ks, Social Security, and life is good. America, what a country! They cannot understand why so many folks are so dumb as to want socialism in the United States.

The two couples ride beside the beach, boardwalk, and ocean. An old man has on a t-shirt that reads "Single Granddad." He is trying to pick up the ladies. The sky is blue and seagulls are abundant and hungry. They stop at a huge gas station for coffee and a snack. A heavy set woman climbs out of the back of an SUV with two dogs.

She is about 60 years old and wears a short yellow dress with high heels. Her anti-virus mask is shiny with fake jewels glued all over it. Her dogs defecate on the grass. Twenty feet away is the Dog Park with a fence around it.

"Hey Lady, why don't you put your shit and your dog shit in the Dog Park?" a young man yells from a car.

The woman puts her cigarette in her mouth and gives him the finger. She is not thinking clearly after a late night of wine and cheese with her thin husband. The SUV has New York tags.

"Do not worry about him. He is not a dog lover. He must be a cat person," Ford said as a joke.

People will step in the dung all day long while talking on cell phones and flossing next to the big parking lot. It is a wonder why she could not figure out where the Dog Park is and go ahead and use it.

"I think it is funny when people wear the mask when they do not need to. That lazy woman with the dogs was out in a field by herself. I like this man-made egg on the biscuit. It is more consistent than real eggs," Dan said.

"I see some people driving their cars all alone wearing a mask. They look like mental patients. What are they thinking?" Candy said.

"The worst is that turkey sausage crap they give you at some hotels. I guess it is cheaper than the real thing and they think you will not notice," Bee said.

"I like beef jerky. My Uncle Phil used to make it when I was a child. He would hunt deer and make it. I guess many people do not like it. He was old and very short, but had a full head of hair. He would eat some jerky and then floss like there was no tomorrow," Candy said.

"We ate beef jerky all the time in the Army. It would not spoil for months and that was nice. I bet the chemicals are not that good for you though. Some soldiers just dangled the stick out of their mouths all day kind of like a cigar," Dan said.

"Many old ladies and men used to chew snuff and tobacco in the south. It would drip down their wrinkled faces at the corners of the mouth. It was so disgusting, but they loved it. They would sit on the porch all day long and enjoy that lifestyle," Candy said.

"We stopped by a Holiday Inn Express in Ohio one time and used the automatic pancake machine. I love those things. The next day it was gone. Someone stole it during the night," Ford said.

"The hungry people are funny darting in and out of the line to get the food early in the morning at those breakfast bars. They will bite off your finger if you get in the way or move too slowly for them. Many wear dirty sleepwear to get breakfast," Bee said.

"Can you guys help me? I got my hog stuck in the sand and cannot move it," a biker asks the brothers.

The biker drove his Ford truck from Pennsylvania with his spotless Breakout in the back. He has three ramps to load and unload it. The trouble is that he must find a ditch or ramp to lower the tailgate so he can load it himself. He found a natural ramp next to the beach, but could not ride his hog through the sand to get it into the truck.

Dan and Ford help him push the hog out of the sand. The biker guns the engine and spins the fat tire and rides it up into the back of the pickup. Sand is flying everywhere.

"I told him to get some help, but he never likes to ask for help. Thank you so much. That thing is so heavy," the wife said.

"Thank you guys. This is the poor man's Breakout. I love your flag and flames custom paint jobs. I am still working on that," the biker said. He pulls away on the beach in his huge, diesel Ford truck in four wheel drive. He does a doughnut for fun. The bumper sticker reads "Someone Forgot to Flush." It has a picture of Joe Biden's head being flushed down a toilet.

A guy pulls up on a jet black Harley Davidson V-rod. His wife rides her own blue V-rod. This is the fastest bike Harley every made with a fat rear tire. The man has a handlebar mustache and tiny round glasses. He grew up in Germany and has worked in the Untied States for twenty years. The husband and wife are both tall and in great shape. They look very strong like gym rats.

"How are you? Those are nice bikes. I love the V-rod. How fast have you had it on the highway?" Ford said.

"Thank you. I had it up to 140 mph once, but that was enough. The ride was very smooth. I was impressed with the Harley-Davidson quality. The BMW bike just does not compare with the Harley look and sound," the German said.

"What kind of work are you into? I bet you are from Austria with that accent. I like it very much. We had Germans in our unit in Kuwait during the war," Dan said.

"I am from Germany. Our team came over here to take over and run an MRI production plant in North Carolina. The previous American team really messed up and was fired en mass," the German said.

"I think I read about that in the paper. The first management team was made up of all Americans. They were dumb and lazy and got fired," Ford said.

"That is pretty much it. The leaders at our headquarters in Germany demand high performance and quality. We turned the plant around quickly and all is well now," the German said.

"The Germans make great machines. That precision is awesome. My friend has a BMW and the quality is amazing. I want to see all those expensive car washes in Germany. They are clean freaks like us," Dan said.

"Do you remember that Otto, Daimler, and Maybach developed the four cycle internal combustion engine in Germany in 1876? Then Karl Benz was the first to commercially make motor vehicles about ten years later. The Germans have a long and glorious history with the awesome internal combustion engine," the wife said.

"I know that history well and love the fossil fuel engine. Now some dumb politicians want to throw it out with the bath water. They believe wild climate projections that are wrong all the time. We should keep improving it and keep rocking and rolling with fossil fuel," Dan said.

"What are the environmental nuts going to do with all the big and useless car batteries when they go bad? That will be really good for the environment. That Harley V-twin is the most awesome example of the internal combustion engine," Ford said.

"We emphasize quality and exports in Germany and Austria. I am surprised that you know about our car wash buildings. My parent's private neighborhood has one that cost $200,000 US dollars. My wife is American and works at the MRI factory also," the German said.

"We ride to Daytona for bike week most years. That is a fun time to get away from work. I love your bikes painted like the ones in Easy Rider. My husband saw that movie in Germany back in the 1970s and fell in love with Harleys," the wife said.

"Yes I did. I wondered if all Americans acted like these characters in the movie. They were into drugs and sex too much. I was glad to find out that most Americans are not like that and work hard. I love the rock and roll though. The Scorpions are from Germany," the husband said.

"I am with you on that. The Scorpions had some great hits. The Easy Rider movie would have been much better with no drugs. The Hollywood folks are really into that crap," Ford said.

They both look German with blond/brown hair and piercing blue eyes. She has long pig tails and a flat stomach. They protect their fair skin from the sun and look to be about fifty years old.

"My father is German and mother American. Do you know where we can get some good barbecue around here? We love that southern barbecue. I grew up in New York and it was hard to find," the wife said.

"We have great barbecue in Lexington, North Carolina where we live now. It is some of the best in the country," the husband said.

"We love barbecue too. I was surprised when we had a shooting contest in Kuwait. Your friends in the German army were not very good at shooting. Their rifles were awesome, but they sucked at marksmanship. We gave them a hard time over alcohol-free beer that night at their camp," Dan said.

"I am not surprised. Most of the smart and educated Germans avoid the military. It is a shame. I served two years and we were strong. Many Germans do not understand that freedom is not free. That is the main reason I am an American citizen now," the German said.

"I am with you on that. This socialism the protesters keep begging for is so stupid. Do they not read history? That is a terrible system for a society," Dan said.

"We had some great barbecue and hush puppies over in Escatawpa. Mary Sue is the server's name. She and her husband own the joint. She said they were devastated in 2005 by Hurricane Katrina. It washed out most of the houses and businesses. That barbecue is the best," Ford said.

"You know that both of you look German. That massive mustache is awesome. I should grow one like that," Dan said.

"You really should grow a big mustache or even a beard. It would break up the monotony of your face. It is brutal to look at you all the time," Ford said.

"He used to cut it very short so it did not go past the corners of his mouth. He looked exactly like Adolph Hitler. I told him to grow it out or we were finished," the wife said.

"She was serious too. I think we need to rustle up many in the media and at the technology companies and put them in jail for lying about Trump and his policies. They are very bad for America and could spark a civil war by promoting socialism and anti-Christian government policies. Many voters should read more, but they do not. Many voters believe the lies and omissions of the media. Most of the media and tech folks are like the socialist Nazi media during the Hitler years," the husband said.

"Take it easy now. We just want to keep America capitalistic, Christian, free, and strong. Have a blessed day now and a great vacation," the wife said.

They speed off on their hogs. Their bikes are built for speed and they dog them on the highway. The wife wears black leather pants and tall boots. They take turns in the lead and love to go fast on a bike or in a car. They stick with German cars and American motorcycles. That makes sense to them.

A biker pulls up on a 2020 Harley Davidson CVO (Custom Vehicle Operations) Street Glide. It is the top of the line version of this model. It is gray and black with orange and red stripes. He has a long, gray beard, black HD t-shirt, and cowboy boots.

"Easy Rider huh? I used to have a thing for the lady at the commune with a knife in her cowgirl boot. She was hot. Daddy would give up red meat for some of that. Your bikes are awesome," the old biker said.

"Thank you. Boy, you have an excellent memory. The hitch hiker was hilarious when he refused to tell Billy where is was from. Where are you from?" Ford said.

"I grew up in Intercourse, Pennsylvania. Can you believe that they named the village that? We tried to change the name to copulation, but the town council would not budge," the old biker said.

"Really? We had lunch there one time at an Amish place. It is near Lancaster and we know the area well. The steak was succulent. We are from Ashland," Dan said.

"We could not believe that the place is named Intercourse. I had to tell my family in China about that village," Bee said.

"There is a village named Intercourse? That is amazing. I never would have dreamed that. They should really change it to coitus or something," Candy said.

"The place was originally named "Cross Keys" in 1754. Two roads crossed there in this community of faith. Intercourse can mean fellowship or Christians helping each other out," the old biker said.

"How about genitalia? Or humpback? Or stimulation? Or Let us Go Together? Or Let us Lie Down Together? Or how about just penetration? I bet the dumb tourists steal the street signs," Ford said.

"And She Was" by the Talking Heads comes on the radio. Dan loves the end of the song when David Byrne makes odd noises like a child.

The old biker has a patch on his leather vest that says "I do not care how you feel: Tell me what you think." Another one says, "No More Bullshit: Trump 2020."

"I love my new bike. It is forty pounds lighter than my 2016 bike. That helps with these old arms and legs at the stop lights. It is so easy to drop one. Have a blessed day," the old biker said.

"I love that CVO! We have the poor man's Harley Davidson Breakout. Your paint job is the top of the line. That thing sparkles. I was told an outside paint shop paints the CVO models for the factory in York. Keep the shiny side up," Dan said.

The old biker removes an official Harley Davidson flask from his backpack. It is covered in black leather with silver rivets. He takes a swig of vodka. The travel flask kit has two shot glasses attached.

"Nik, Nik, Nik! I knew you would like that," the old biker said as he flaps his arm up and down. He is quoting from his favorite movie Easy Rider.

The old biker does a burn out and the CVO roars. His long beard blows in the wind. You can tell by looking at his bike that you could be comfortable for days riding it across the country. The quality is very impressive. The factory folks remove most of the vibration for the rider's arms, hands, feet, and butt. The Honda factory folks in Japan do that too, but just cannot replicate the look and sound of the legendary American Harley Davidson. The biker has a huge eagle on the back of his jacket.

"Did you say you picture yourself as an eagle? I wonder if you would be dumb like a deer and not prepare for winter by gathering food. Or would you be smart like a squirrel and collect acorns to eat during the winter? I bet you would eat like a pig and not prepare for winter meals," Bee said.

"You are so sweet baby. I picture myself as an eagle or perhaps a big, strong lion. I never miss a meal and would prepare my winter meals in advance for sure. I would ensure a variety of nuts and berries for myself," Dan said.

"You are full of something. You are more like a headless fly. They move around without any plan for the day or week. They eat dung you know. That is definitely you baby. I have noticed that you never miss a meal. I think everyone has noticed," Bee said.

"I forgot to ask you about the golf tournament last week. Who won that one at Saint Simons Island? I was out riding hogs with crazy Phil. He showed me where he fell out of the deer stand," Dan said.

"That was a good one. Streb beat Kisner in a playoff. Streb almost holed it from the fairway on 18 for an eagle on the par four. It was awesome," Ford said.

"That sucks that I missed a playoff. I love a playoff. I bet when those guys get old they will look back and be so proud that they were so strong and great at that game. I bet they will not believe that they could do that in their youth. I know I would be that way," Dan said.

"I can see you kind of like Jimmy Demaret. He won the Masters three times, but the Augusta

National Golf Club members never talk about him. He wore bright, funny clothes, sang in a funny voice, and performed stand up comedy. He was awesome in shorts during a tournament just to entertain the fans! He was on I Love Lucy in 1954. The club should really honor him this year at the Masters," Ford said.

"Unchained" by Van Halen comes on the stereo. Dan and Ford are in awe of Eddie Van Halen who died this year. Eddie fooled his piano teacher as a kid for years that he could read music. The teacher busted him when Eddie had to turn pages while the teacher played the piano in concert. He did not know when to turn the page and the teacher was disappointed in little Eddie. RIP Eddie Van Halen!

Chapter Six
The Old Bikers Enjoy Louisiana

The two couples are riding down the four-lane state highway enjoying the breeze and the sites. They see many small frame houses with odd stuff in the yards. There are five foot metal chickens, old and rusted appliances, and huge blow-up figures laying flat on the grass waiting for sunset to be inflated again.

An old school bus with the city name blacked out passes the bikers. Twenty migrants from Florida are in the bus going back home from Pennsylvania. They help with the tomato crop up there every year.

The migrants are hard workers and love America. They are smiling, laughing, and watching Bee, Dan, Candy, and Ford rolling down the road. The hogs are so bright and colorful and the workers love it. They give the thumbs up at this depiction of American freedom. They can hear the roar of the American made Harley engines. The chrome wheels almost blind the migrants.

The team leader blows the bus horn in approval. He bought the bus and supervises the group while they are working in the fields in Pennsylvania. The workers send most of their wages home to their wives and children in Central and South America. They love the American dream and America loves them. Dan and Ford dog their motorcycles to entertain the hard workers going home. The migrants are in a great mood with a pocket full of dough after a summer of hard work.

The migrants dream of the day they can afford a nice car, house, and motorcycle. They are content now with the apartments, loving families, and jobs. They make triple the wages that they would make in their native countries. They are proud that they came to America legally and cannot believe how well they live here. They do not understand the protesters, rioters, and looters in the big cities and would never support them in any way. They all believe in God, Jesus, and The Bible.

The four bikers ride over to Citizens Cemetery in Picayune, Louisiana. Dan read about the place online and thought it would be fun to walk around and read the old gravestones. It appears that nobody mows the grass here. The weeds and small trees have taken the cemetery hostage. Some trees died a long time ago and lean on other trees.

"What does that one say? Many of these people died young back then. I guess health care was non-existent," Dan said.

"This woman died in 1896 at age 36. Her name is Hettie Burkhart. I guess her child died at two years old also. It tells when the baby died," Bee said.

Dan and Ford glance back at the flag bike and the flames bike shining in the afternoon sun. They will take some pictures of the bikes in front of this cemetery and all the moss hanging from the trees.

Many tombstones are crooked, cracked, and illegible after being here over one hundred years. Some head stones are lying flat on the weeds and ferns.

"I wonder why volunteers do not keep this place clean. It seems like someone would take care of this burial ground. Maybe nobody visits their relatives here," Candy said.

The people with money bought tall spires and mausoleums to honor themselves. The poor folks have small tombstones that cannot be read due to erosion. Some simply say mother, father, and baby died on so and so date.

"The dead folks buried here must be furious that their descendants do not keep the cemetery mowed and respectable. I bet some of the descendants enjoyed the inheritance and forgot about the people who left them that free money," Ford said.

Some of the tombstones are humorous with the following written on them, "I told you I was sick, Merv Smith- Greatest Fisherman, Walter Stone- He loved to spend money, but he had none, and Maureen Jones- Woman of 1000 Voices."

Some families bought heavy stones and chain to fence in their family plots. Many of the stones are sinking into the dirt and most of the chains fell down many years ago.

"I want to be cremated. I do not trust anyone to care after our mausoleum. Ashes thrown into the ocean would be just fine," Bee said.

"I agree with that. These funeral homes and others make a fortune off the dead and their survivors," Ford said.

"How about those sick criminals down in Jacksonville? They attempted to dig up Ronnie Van Zant and his family had to exhume his corpse and bury it under a huge concrete block. Lynyrd Skynyrd was awesome," Dan said.

Dan starts singing "Sweet Home Alabama" while walking back to the Easy Rider bikes. He loves how long and low they are. He wonders if a fatter tire could fit on the rear.

Three people pull up in a Chevy truck. "Ramblin Man" from the Allman Brothers is playing in the truck. They walk into the cemetery. They carry US flags and real flowers. It is a married couple and their teenage girl. They clean tombstones and ground around them. They remember these people with profound respect and love.

The bikers hope that their families and friends do the same for them when they are gone. They try to be nice and better people for the next few days, but it is hard to sustain with so many jerks around.

An old lady walks up to the bikers. She is thin and looks tough. She has big muscles covered in flannel and worn blue jeans. She sweeps debris off several graves while whistling "Free Bird" by Lynyrd Skynyrd between sips of coffee.

"Good day to you. Can you believe that one cup of coffee costs four duckies nowadays? That is unbelievable," the old woman said.

"I know it is outrageous. You take me back to southern Virginia and the Carolinas with the slang word duckie. I got that from a girl named Mary Temple back in the 1970s. The Federal Reserve fools have been printing money like crazy for the last few decades and that has created inflation. You are so sweet to clean the graves of your relatives," Dan said.

"Really? We used that word duckie all the time growing up in Hilton Head. I still hear it every week around here. We help clean the entire cemetery these days. It really needs it. May God bless you and your family now," the old lady said.

"This place could be so nice with some upkeep. It is beautiful down here. I wonder why the owner does not clean and mow and fix up the place," Ford said.

"The couple who owned this cemetery inherited it from his father. They got addicted to drugs and alcohol and filed for bankruptcy last year. They leased brand new Cadillacs every two years until the money ran out. I hope a Christian person buys this place soon and fixes it up. We try to do our part," the old lady said.

"Did you know that the University of Missouri had to put an acrylic case around Thomas Jefferson's original headstone from

1833? It is from Monticello in Virginia. Some leftist idiots were threatening to destroy it. The case costs $20,000 of tax money," Dan said.

"There is no excuse for that. These protesters need to read just a little bit of history and realize how great America really is now compared to other nations. We should dip them in wax and make them get a job," Ford said.

"I love TJ's quote about the fact that he does not care if you have one God or fifty. Just let us live in peace side by side and let us have freedom of religion," Dan said.

"My friend Dennis in Virginia is obsessed with Thomas Jefferson. He rides his Harley Davidson Deluxe to Monticello every week and has an annual pass to the grounds. He has a TJ tattoo. Even his wife thinks he is a nut," Ford said.

"I bet TJ would have a fit if he knew how big and controlling our government is now. He would shoot down a surveillance drone if it flew over Monticello," Dan said.

"This headstone is for Aunt Baby. I think Seinfeld did a bit about that. Frank Costanza spoke about her," Bee said.

"These two siblings died on the same day. The head stone reads May 24, 1890. One lived to be 22 and the other 24. That is so sad. We live so long now. Maybe they had a terrible accident. Perhaps we live too long these days," Candy said.

An old biker woman pulls up in a bright red Smart car with a huge Harley-Davidson Women sticker on the rear window. A life-size cardboard cutout figure of Kris Kristofferson is in the passenger seat with the seat belt on. The tag reads "MP." She is from South Carolina. At a glance, it looks like a real person in the passenger seat.

"I love that Smart car. Is the quality good? Who is that riding shotgun? Is that Waylon Jennings? I loved his music," Dan said.

"Thank you sugar. I love Smart cars and the quality is great. The Mercedes folks really know how to build a car. That is Kris Kristofferson of course. We have been involved since the special concert in Richmond in 2008. He is very special to me," MP said.

The Kristofferson super fan has a tattoo on her arm that reads "KK=MP Forever." She said that her third husband never understood her relationship with the musician, but the fourth husband is okay with it. He thinks it is cute and harmless.

The four bikers leave Picayune and roll down Interstate 59 toward New Orleans. They cross over the bridge on Lake Pontchartrain. The lake and sky are blue and beautiful. Dan and Ford have fun passing each other and dogging their hogs.

They stop just over the massive bridge in the parking lot. Many men and women are fishing off the bridge. Some folks are having a picnic. One guy is playing "Lonely Is The Night" by Billy Squier really loud.

"Are you catching anything? I bet the fish are huge down here. I saw Billy Squier twice in concert back in the 1980s and 1990s. He was awesome," Dan said.

"No, nothing is biting today. I love the rock and roll too. Those are some nice bikes. You must love Easy Rider. We love it too," the fisherman said.

"Thank you. My brother and I always wanted to paint some hogs like Wyatt and Billy's. We finally got around to it," Ford said.

"I bought a CVO Breakout and rode it home to show the wife a while back. She did not go for it and made me return it. I felt like a fool. I love the Breakout. It reminds me of the Rocker," the fisherman said.

"Hang in there. I am sure that you can ride again my man. I hope the fish start biting. Take it easy," Dan said.

"Lay It On The Line" by Triumph comes on a radio. Ford thinks about the awesome US Festival in 1983 in southern California. He could not make it, but bought the concert DVD. Many great bands played that weekend. Wozniak, the Apple guy, paid for the concert.

Ford sees the huge crowd at the concert in his mind. There must have been 500,000 mostly young folks having a great time at the show. They were so full of life on those 96 degree days in the California sun. He thinks about all the great concerts he attended back in the 1970s and 1980s.

"I was coming on strong and then the virus hit and we all got laid off. My old lady left town with a country singer named Bobby with bad credit. That sucks. I hope they make it," the fisherman said.

"I bet the catfish are yummy. We have not had those in a long time. Cracker Barrel used to have good catfish," Bee said.

"We used to catch and eat turtles and catfish all the time when I was a kid down here. We would saute them in a pan in the kitchen with many spices," Candy said.

"Bobby, the country singer, left this awesome belt and buckle from Nashville by mistake. It must be worth $500. I cannot wait to get back to work, get the kids some clothes, and buy a Breakout from Harley-Davidson," the fisherman said.

"Here is a little something for you and the kids. God bless you and your family my man. Stay strong in the good old USA," Ford said. He slips the fisherman $50 for no reason. The fisherman grins ear to ear.

"Thank you. Thank you. Thank you mister. You are the best. I love your bikes with the flames and US flag. Have a safe vacation and ride now. God bless you," the fisherman said.

The fisherman wears a Led Zeppelin t-shirt. He usually catches some fish for lunch and dinner with his family and friends every few days. The view from the bridge is spectacular and they have a good time. "Immigrant Song" by Led Zeppelin comes on the cell phone and the fishermen play air guitar.

Dan wraps up the conversation due to intestinal pressure that is building. He usually has napkins in his pockets for the mother load. He walks behind some trees and lets it out. He buries the waste with a tree limb.

"Do not tell me about it. You are disgusting. Why can't you be normal? Why can't you be smart? I see an outhouse over there," Bee said.

"I would rather use the woods. We used to dig cat holes all the time in the Army. It is kind of nice. The fresh air is wonderful baby," Dan said.

A fisherman packs up his fishing pole and tackle box on his Sportster. He does a few donuts in the grass next to the bridge. Everyone enjoys this show. His bike is from 2004 and has a carburetor with a slow idle. It sounds great with straight pipes and no baffles. He dogs it while getting back on the highway.

"I just read that the Army canceled the shark attack. This bunch at the Pentagon is getting soft and I am worried," Dan said.

"What is the shark attack? I do not remember you telling me about that one," Bee said.

"The drill sergeants used to yell at the trainees when you got off the bus at basic training. It creates stress and chaos kind of like being in combat. I really enjoyed it and laughed so much that day at Fort Jackson in 1984," Dan said.

"What do they do now? They must talk about their feelings and about being victims," Bee said.

"I bet you are right. This crap of treating people like babies is not good for anyone. Did you know that 60% of American colleges do not require a standardized test now? That is ridiculous. Ignorance is pervasive in our society now," Dan said.

"We must read about history to ensure our freedom and capitalism. There will always be many fools in government, big business, the media, big tech, and colleges who love socialism and big and corrupt government. They are terrible for America," Ford said.

The bikers leave the bridge and ride to a big steakhouse. The summer air feels so good rolling down the highway. The t-bones and rib-eyes are huge with more fat than usual. The folks try to put the Wuhan virus situation in the back of their minds.

The two couples bow their heads to God. Ford says a prayer for the group to God and Jesus for everything. There is no begging. He only thanks God for everything right in the world. Every day they are reminded how lucky they are to be successful and rich in the free and great United States of America.

"Have you noticed that cow and pig prices have come down? I read that the ranchers had too many animals this spring and summer due to lower demand. Many cows gained 100 extra pounds munching the feed on the farms. That is awesome," Dan said.

"I love it. This steak is the best one I ever had. Look at this baby. Let us dine on cow tomorrow also. Pig and chicken are out on this trip," Ford said.

"We could never afford steak when I was growing up. We had hamburger and chicken most weeks. My parents should not have had children. They should die. Oh, they did die," Candy said.

"I love your name. Is Candy your real name or a nickname?" Bee said.

"My real name is Candace. I never liked long names. People just call me Candy. It just stuck as a kid," Candy said.

"I hope they cook the meat enough. I had salmonella a while back during my celibate period. It was a long, long celibate period. I was fat, ugly, and dumb and the ladies did not want it," Ford said.

"Boy, you can talk some trash. What are you talking about? I know you did not have salmonella," Candy said.

Ford leaves the young server a tip of $100. She is in college and money is very tight. She is smiling and laughing while telling the other servers about her good fortune today.

Bee, Dan, Candy, and Ford walk around in the steakhouse parking lot flossing. That was the best meal of the trip. The bill was $200 for the four of them and worth every penny. The money and good times are flowing.

Dan and Ford rev up their mean machines and scream onto the highway. Their tummies are full and the bikers are feeling fine. Four smiles roll down the road on the chrome horses made by Harley-Davidson.

The two couples rent bicycles in the French Quarter in New Orleans. It is not as crowded as usual due to the virus going around. Riding bicycles reminds them of being children so long ago. Dan spots Herman the Clown sitting on his trike on Decatur Street and stops for a chat.

"Hey, I saw you at Daytona Beach Bike Week last year. How are you? I like your trike," Dan said.

"Hello there. Yes, that was a good time. They let me be a judge for the bikini contest down there on Main Street. Check this out," Herman said.

He pulls out his cellphone and Sir-Mix-a-Lot's song "Baby Got Back" begins to play. A video plays showing the contestants in the bikini contest from the rear of course. Some of the butts are large and some are perfect size. The clown obviously loves the young ladies. One contestant was short, old, and wrinkled.

"This one was the winner. Boy she had it all. I got a big hug from her and all the sexy, young ladies. Were you down there at the beach?" Herman said.

"We drove down for the last week. That is a wild time down there close to The Boot Hill Saloon. The bikers are so funny to watch," Ford said.

There is a big difference between a regular clown and a biker clown. It is indistinguishable to the untrained eye. One is nice and normal and one is too horny and wild.

Herman's trike is made of parts from Harley Davidsons, Nortons, Indians, and Volkswagons. He and a friend built it on a Honda frame. There is a huge stuffed werewolf siting on the rear bench seat. He is ready for Halloween.

A couple with two kids walk by. The little girl starts crying and tries to hit Herman with her candy cane. The costume or the smell frightened her. He smells like a cigar and body odor.

"This pandemic has really hurt my business. The kids are afraid of clowns and the parents are too. They think they are going to get sick from the virus," Herman said.

"That is too bad. Hopefully, we will have a vaccine soon. Are you married?" Dan said.

"Yes, but my old lady does not like the biker rallies. I go alone and as long I bring home some money or jewelry she is happy," Herman said.

"I hope she does not leave you for a younger clown. That would be a tragedy my man. We do not see clowns very often in Pennsylvania," Ford said.

"You have that right. I have been doing this for 34 years and my balls are sagging for sure. My grandfather was a clown in Oklahoma City many years ago. He was very popular over there," Herman said.

Candy, Ford, Bee, and Dan lock the bicycles and walk around in Jackson Square. There are street performers trying to make a buck. They run and do flips. They take turns passing a bucket for tips. Most tourists ignore them and keep their dough. Their talent does not impress most strangers.

"I bet his wife woke up one day and said oh my God, I am married to a clown. I wonder if she was okay with him doing that job full time," Candy said.

"That is an odd career field. I wonder if he makes good money doing that. His outfit was too dirty and stinky," Bee said.

"He said that he makes $80 for a day and gets free beer. He tells jokes and wears a strap-on dildo sometimes. He is quite a showman," Dan said.

"He might want to think about changing his clown name. I have never heard of a clown with the name Herman. He said he is heading to the bike rally in Panama City, Florida," Bee said.

All of a sudden the organ on top of the steamboat begins to play. It is very loud. An old woman has been playing on the ship for decades. She is very talented and the tourists love the music. The Mississippi River is wide and beautiful. Aggressive birds are flying and walking around scrounging for free food from the tourists.

They read the signs about how Andrew Jackson and the US Army defeated the British in the Battle of New Orleans in 1815. They have some ice cream and enjoy the sites.

"That Andrew Jackson was awesome. He had open houses in the White House in 1830 and did not care about the more educated fools who looked down on the common man. He ignored the Supreme Court sometimes. We should ignore the Supreme Court idiots when they ignore our constitution," Ford said.

"I know, he did a lot of good. Trump reminds me of him with that outsider attitude and sticking up for the common man. That

Obamacare welfare crap is obviously unconstitutional," Dan said.

"Trump is hilarious at the rallies. He is like a standup comedian for sure. I am glad he stands for capitalism and not that horrible socialism or communism. That crap has really hurt the normal, hardworking Chinese people," Bee said.

"Look at that guy. He can really dance and jump. They look like brothers," Candy said.

Five guys are running, jumping, and dancing for cash. They play hip hop music and try to hustle the crowd. They sport many tattoos and piercings.

"We need to play golf my brother. I saw a Masters shirt on a guy back there. Do you remember that Chamber of Commerce team event where I carried you all day? You really sucked," Dan said.

"I remember you being a boat anchor. That is what I remember my useless brother. You really sucked that day. You should have just been my caddie and driven the cart," Ford said.

"That was devasting when the Masters was canceled back in April due to the Wuhan virus. I look forward to that tournament so much. At least we can watch it in November," Dan said.

"I know, that golf course is so beautiful with the trees, plants, and flowers all around. They run a tight ship on that 400 acres. Do you remember when brother Al got thrown out for talking on a cell phone in the woods beside number 13?" Ford said.

"That was hilarious. He had to walk two miles back to the car to leave the phone and then back to the course. The security guard looked like Barney Fife on the Andy Griffith show. He was so proud of the arrest," Dan said.

The bikers ride the bicycles back to he New Orleans Visitor Center where they parked the hogs. Dan's bike seat is too low and it is a children's bike. It was all they had left at the rental stand.

Ford has to use the bathroom. He walks into the very nice visitor center and finds the only stall surrounded by police tape. There is a leak and the plumber is on the way. The stall door is locked with a chain. He must use the toilet and climbs over the wall and accomplishes his mission. The toilet sounds like a jet engine.

"Have a nice day," the receptionist said to Ford with a big smile. She is a retired school teacher and works two days per week in the lobby for fun. She knows what he did and smiles because her husband would have done the same thing in a pinch. She does wonder if he climbed under the stall or over it.

Ford does not care what anyone thinks of his persistence and creativity in getting to the toilet. He was in a hurry and flushed twice. He has a pep in his step on the way back to the others in the parking lot. He whistles and sings, "L.A. Woman" by the Doors.

They ride hogs back to the campground in Biloxi on Highway 10. Traffic is light and they get up to 90 mph on the motorcycles. They pass a bus full of Catholic nuns. All the nuns are waving and smiling at the bikers. They love to get out.

They sit outside the cabins and dine on food from the small restaurant. The view is beautiful of the beach and ocean. Some folks are riding bikes and walking on the concrete boardwalk across the highway. Several bikers cruise by on big Harley-Davidsons. Some are speeding and some take their time. One guy has a tall American flag on the back of his hog.

"You know I met a guy one time who had a warranty claim denied by Harley for a huge American flag on the back of his trike. The factory denied the claim because the flag and pole put too much stress on the transmission. The jury is still out on that flag mounting and claim denial," Dan said.

"I wonder why the government employees put up the county signs everywhere. Who cares when you drive from one county to another? How much tax money do they spend on that crap?" Ford said.

"I have always wondered about that too. There are about 3,100 counties in the United States. Perhaps government is too big now? The government folks waste so much tax money," Bee said.

"I wish the politicians would stop wasting so much money on mulch, trees, and flowers on the highways and streets. The workers have a lot of tax taken out of their checks for that crap," Candy said.

"Remind me to put new shoes on our Honda Civic when we get back home. I will forget and the tread is getting bare. I love new shoes on the car. That is what rednecks say," Dan said.

"That is what you say. New shoes? Every time you go away on the motorcycle you start talking like a redneck. Please be normal. They are not shoes. They are called tires," Bee said.

"My whole family talks like that. I would know exactly what he was saying with the shoes for vehicles. I love to hear different slang words and phrases in different states," Candy said.

"Dan is a shagwa. That means dumb melon head in China. I love slang like that. I guess it is my social responsibility to take care of him and help him make good decisions," Bee said.

They notice twenty Arab women bikers a few doors down at their cabins in the campground. This is an odd and welcome sight. Only about 20% of US bikers are female and that is a shame. A Harley Davidson Road King has a three foot cream stuffed bear tied onto the sissy bar. The bear has a sausage biscuit in his mouth.

"Where are you from? I see that you have these very nice rental bikes. It is so great to see all the women riding. It was very rare to see a woman ride her own bike when I was young," Ford said.

"We are from Saudi Arabia. Our government just allowed us to drive cars and motorcycles during 2018 and we are so thrilled to do it. We flew in for the bike rally in Panama City Beach," Leen said.

"She is the pretty team leader who planned the entire trip. She told me that her husband is a member of the Royal family. I read online that the House of Saud was founded in 1720 and comprised of about 15,000 mostly overweight and lazy people," Candy told Ford.

"Do you know why the bear is eating pig? The bear represents our king behaving badly. Most people in our country think pigs are unclean and will not eat them. We will remove the pig from his mouth when he gives us equal rights just as the American women have here. We love your freedom," another women said.

"That is fantastic! I read about the old king and young prince easing up on the control freak laws. American women would not put up with it. Do not put up with fools. It took 144 years for our male fools to be overridden so women could vote. God is great!" Dan said.

"We love freedom and love America. Our dumb government people still require the abaya (head to toe dress) to be worn while riding the bike, but we cheat and do not wear it. We are fighting every day for equal rights in our country, but it is tough," Leen said.

"You are so strong. The men in China thought they were more important than women when I was growing up. That is the main reason I came to America for citizenship twenty years ago. Everyone is the same in the United States, thank God," Bee said.

"Yes, I cannot believe that you have to put up with that crap from stupid men. God bless you for standing up. You look awesome riding those bikes. Men are the worst," Candy said.

"Let us go out for sausage biscuits tomorrow morning for breakfast. McDonald's has the best. I love the pig. They are so cute. Our pigs in this nation are very clean," Ford said.

The Saudi women wear jeans and summer sweaters with long and flowing jet black hair. A few have on head scarves, but not many. They are enjoying the time away from the old fashioned men in their home country. Some wear t-shirts. Their jewelry looks expensive. Some sport high heels and others biker boots.

"We flew into New York City from Riyadh and shopped at the Tiffany store. We saw Melania come out of Trump Tower. That was fabulous. She is so beautiful and strong," Leen said.

"Boy, that king of Thailand is wild with the harem. He is very frisky. I read that he has a sleeve tattoo. They need to take that crown and allowance and make my boy get a real job. I thank God that the United States has never had a stupid king and queen and never will," Dan said.

"I am your queen. You should bow down to me when you enter my room. That would be great. Can you do that? I am from heaven and a perfect person," Bee said to Dan.

"I must ask you a question. Why do the people protest in your streets for equal rights and freedom? America is the beacon of freedom for the world. The United States is the top symbol of freedom and equal rights on the planet. Can these protesters read? We see people doing whatever they want in your country every day. They should try to live in our country. I cannot even get a divorce from my bad husband," Leen said.

"Most of those protesters and rioters want free stuff. Many do not like to work and are criminals. You are correct that all it takes to be successful in America is some learning and hard work. Our federal, state, and local laws ensure equal rights," Dan said.

The Saudi women mention that they love to dine on lamb. The next day Ford burns $3,000 for a huge lamb brunch to honor the visitors. He brought in a big caterer from New Orleans. There is a huge party tent erected at the campground with roasted and juicy lamb, jelly, sauces, pastries, salad, artichoke, and cake. A good time was had by all.

The group of 24 bikers ride over to Mobile, Alabama after the catered brunch for fun.

Several Saudi bikers video the whole ride. Leen and Dan switch bikes for a while rolling down Highway 10. Leen looks so strong and proud riding the flag Breakout. Bee and Dan ride her Road King in style. Candy and Ford switch bikes with another Saudi woman so she can strut her stuff on the flames Breakout.

Ford is singing "Sweet Child o' Mine" by Guns and Roses to himself rolling down the interstate. Dan is singing "Welcome To The Jungle" by the same folks. They love the beat, excellent guitar work, and funny lyrics and the sound of all the Harleys. The Saudi ladies research and read the lyrics on their phones to many crazy rock and roll songs. They ask the Americans to interpret the meaning. The Americans use so many different words to describe the same thing.

They take pictures and have a great time over coffee and tea. They tour an old Spanish fort near Pascagoula on the way back. The Saudis and the Americans climb the fort walls and run around like children. Their enjoyment of freedom is infectious for everyone at the tourist attraction. Children run and play with the ladies. Candy, Bee, Dan, and Ford realize that the visitors could never act or dress like this at home in the kingdom.

The group ride their hogs onto the ferry that services Fort Massachusetts in the Gulf of Mexico. It is on Ship Island, a tiny island about ten miles out. The United States began planning a fort here beginning after the War of 1812. Construction began in 1859 under the supervision of the Army Corps of Engineers.

Leen whips out her American Express card before Dan has a chance to pay for the ferry ride for everyone. The Harleys look awesome, brand new, and bright on the ferry. The day is blessed with blue sky and puffy white clouds. They watch dolphins and see beautiful uninhabited islands on the way.

Candy and Bee try on the headscarves while riding on the ferry. They are made of silk, wool, and cashmere and cost thousands of dollars. Bee's favorite is bright red, yellow, and orange. It was handmade in northern Italy. Candy loves the white and red scarf with red hearts on it made of the finest cashmere from Mongolia. It was handmade in an old house in Athens, Greece. The Saudis give the scarves to Bee and Candy as gifts.

"I guess those European women dodged a bullet in 1683 when the Hapsburg army defeated the Ottomans. They could have been ruled by

Muslims for centuries and denied equal rights for a long, long time," Dan said.

"That is correct. We know that history also and want women to have equal rights everywhere. As you know, the Turks and Iranians or Persians cause trouble sometimes for the Arab nations like mine. The Turks threaten to stop the Euphrates River from flowing south to our allies and families," Leen said.

"That dictator-want-to-be in Turkey should die! He should die! He looks like a little girl chicken," another Saudi said.

"Well that is nice. You live in a rough neighborhood for sure. He reminds me of the oh so weak Biden hiding in his basement. They both look like female chickens or hens with tiny legs and weak calves. That is not a good look for a man," Dan said.

"My brother wanted to be a woman back in high school, but I talked him out of it. He still enjoys clothing with flowers, pinks, and pastels though," Ford said.

"Do not pay attention to him. He is only joking around. He ate paint chips as a child," Dan said.

"He can have this Burberry silk scarf to make his fashion statement. It is for men and women.

It goes perfectly with his Harley Davidson black t-shirt," Leen said.

"I do love that red, yellow, and orange scarf. We pray for your equal rights in your home country. You are always welcome here in the awesome and free United States of America. Come visit us on the farm in Pennsylvania any time. We have plenty of room in our guest house or barn," Dan said.

"Thank you very much for your friendship and kindness. We love America. Our backward nation did not get rid of slavery until 1962. Can you believe that? We will come visit you when we gain equal rights for women in Saudi Arabia. We have tremendous guest houses in Riyadh if you can come visit," Leen said.

The group rides back to the campground. They take turns playing music from Saudi Arabia and America on the boombox. They chat late into the night. The hogs sparkle in the fire light. Dan wears a colorful scarf around his neck for entertainment.

Candy, Bee, Ford, and Dan ride to an unofficial hog shop the next day. There are many of these repair shops in the United States that are totally independent from the Harley Davidson Motor Company. Ford spots this one on the side of the highway. The owner has a skeleton on an old rusted Harley as his street sign.

They walk into the dimly lit shop and see a glass tank full of snakes. A woman with many tattoos is trying to catch one with a stick.

"Welcome to Dirt's Place. How may I help you? Where are you from? I love the paint on those bikes," the woman said.

"Thank you. We just wanted to look around and check out those choppers outside. We are from Ashland, Pennsylvania. They look very nice with the raked out front ends and fat tires," Ford said.

"That sounds great. We have a few very nice used hogs for sale. Dirt! Dirt we have some customers. Get your ass out here," the wife said.

"Why do you call him Dirt? Does he like to play in the dirt? That must be a nickname," Dan said.

"Oh, no, his name is Donald Ray Thomas. His nickname Dirt is based on that. Can you believe it? His own mother came up with that nickname. She is a bad person. She is a piece of crap. Somebody hit her with the ugly stick," the wife said.

Dirt walks out of the back covered in oil and grease. He has more tattoos than his wife. He is very friendly and proud to have his own shop.

He used to work at an official Harley shop, but had a falling out with the owner's lazy son. He smokes a pipe.

"Hello there! You must love that old movie Easy Rider. I do too. That looks awesome on your bikes. How about a snake? The old lady got carried away collecting them on our land," Dirt said.

"No thank you. We do not like snakes up in Pennsylvania and kill them every chance we get. You have some pretty ones though. Boy, that one is so long," Dan said.

Dirt has an odd habit of rubbing and scratching around his nose with his fingers and the back side of his hand. It appears to the casual observer that he is going to pick his nose, but he never does. People watch for the pick, but it never comes. Sometimes the finger touches the nostril, but never penetrates.

"I read that many people worship snakes in Africa. The Maasai society is ruled by men and they love snakes. They raise cows and children to increase their wealth. The more the better in the man's tiny brain. If the dumb men have plenty of one, but not the other, they are considered poor," Bee said.

"Let us visit Kenya and watch these folks with the snakes, cows, and many children running around. That would be a great vacation now because the virus made all the prices drop down in Africa," Dan said.

"You can go. Do not call me! That sounds horrible. Can you imagine the body odor? You are not right. Can I get a boyfriend if you go down to Africa? Don't call us. We will be in the swimming pool," Bee said.

"Bee is right. I bet they do not sell floss down there. How will you cope with that? You would come home with rotten teeth and weighing 300 pounds. You would have big chunks of food in your teeth," Ford said.

"You would come back like that guy from Allentown working at the dog biscuit factory in the newspaper. The team leader noticed his biscuit production went down by half and suspected a thief. The video cameras caught this hungry employee eating the biscuits. He was arrested for eating about half of the biscuits coming down the conveyor belt. He was huge and did not even have a dog. You would do that," Dan said.

"You are right. I bet they have the same problem at the Hershey factory near us. Much of the candy is small and folks love it. I have noticed that the average person in Hershey is larger than the general population of the state," Ford said.

"I would love to see the women balancing the huge baskets on their heads. The women look so strong on the TV shows from Africa. I guess many tribes still hate each other in many cases and fight each other," Candy said.

"You are correct. Some of the men steal cows from rival tribes to increase their wealth. It can lead to horrible violence. Some of the tribal people still eat monkeys," Bee said.

The four bikers enjoy a delicious meal at the Outback and then sit around the campfire at the campground. "Clap For The Wolfman" by The Guess Who comes on the radio. Dan and Ford remember Wolfman Jack broadcasting from Mexico back in the 1960s and 1970s great rock and roll and blues songs.

"Do you remember that guy? The border radio stations broadcasted at 250,000 watts or five times the limit in the United States back then. We could pick up the Wolfman from coast to coast back in our youth on those family trips," Ford said.

"Yes, it was like SiriusXM satellite radio without the satellites. Those were good times listening to the Wolfman. He could talk some trash," Dan said.

"Do you know he died in North Carolina about 1995. He was awesome! He had a house in Belvidere for some reason. Can you imagine running into the Wolfman at the grocery store in North Carolina?" Ford said.

They throw out weird or funny topics to get a reaction. All four love this game. They pretend that corporate employees brainstorm and come up with some odd, yet real products.

"How about the corporate meeting that launched the underwear? The guy in the corner stands up with his brilliant idea to wear clothes under his clothes.

"Let us manufacture and sell under garments to folks with no dough. They are totally unnecessary, but will be a big hit," Dan said.

"You are right, they are unnecessary for sure. Why do you need two layers?" Candy said.

"I think the people in Japan or Hawaii invented the leather loincloth about 7,000 years ago. I guess they wanted to wear diapers," Ford said.

"How about the nut who suggested cigarettes? He ingests smoke into his lungs, chokes like crazy, and really enjoys the whole experience," Ford said.

"I have this idea of starting a small fire in my hand and inhaling the smoke from the fire. It makes it hard to breathe, but other than that it is very exciting. We call it the cigarette," the idiot at the meeting said.

"What a moron that guy must have been. How can people do that? Filling up your lungs with smoke is a bad idea for sure. Most men in China still smoke cigarettes. They are the worst," Bee said.

"I think the people down in Mexico invented cigarettes during the 9th century. I bet they got a buzz on them," Candy said.

"How about the person who came up with four years of free college? That was brilliant for the student, but not so brilliant for the parent and their bank account or the poor taxpayers," Ford said.

"Let us build these very nice little villages for our young and lazy citizens. We will get their parents to pay for everything for years. We will insulate them from failure and poverty. They will learn so much about this world and we will get rich. We will allow them to protest about dumb stuff they do not understand all the time. This will be great," the dumb college leader said.

"I guess the original colleges were all about God and Jesus and the Bible. They did not put up with drunken, dumb, horny, or lazy students as they do today. These youngsters have it made today," Candy said.

"I propose a law that only taxpayers can protest or beg the dumb politicians for tax money. I further proclaim that only landowners can vote. That is the way things used to be when those geniuses founded this awesome country in 1776. Let us go back to that system," Dan said.

"That is a grand idea. Did you know that only 48% of adults in America pay any federal income tax now? That is terrible to have all the free loaders. Most of them do not care if the stupid federal politicians bankrupt the country as long as they get free stuff now," Ford said.

"You reminded of that famous Bible with the misprint. A church printed hundreds of Bibles in 1631 that said, "Thou shalt commit adultery," Bee said.

"Wow, I bet somebody got forty lashes for that one. Perhaps they were stretched on one of those wooden tables. Maybe they were boiled in oil like that kid who criticized the Catholic church Pope, leaders, and doctrine," Dan said.

Candy, Bee, Ford, and Dan ride hogs back up to Ashland, Pennsylvania from New Orleans. They only have two rainy days and have so much fun. The ride is 1,200 miles and the only problem is that their butts get sore and numb.

They love the open road and freedom and just being together. Ford's profit from the Corvette deal is flowing like a river. They stop every 80-90 miles and walk around. They take their time getting back home. There are many odd meals and snacks along the way. Candy decided to ride back with Ford and move into his fine farm house. They are an item now.

The first thing Candy notices at Ford's farm is the big American flag blowing in the breeze on the red and white barn. She agrees that all barns should be red and white. Ford carries Candy across the threshold on his covered porch to pretend that they just got married. She is impressed with his big, two-story house and twenty acres. He is so happy to have found someone to share his life.

Candy has heard Ford and Dan tease each other over who bought the first farm for cash and who has more acres. The brothers have figured out how to work hard, make a ton of money, and pay cash for a 12 acre farm and one 20 acre farm. Candy and Ford will make it. There is no doubt that they are a perfect match for life.

Candy loves the way both Ford and Dan put their ladies on a pedestal. They learned to be gentlemen from their loving Grandmother. They called her MaMa and she had a strong influence on both of them. They open doors and pay attention to others' needs. MaMa was full of love and loved to teach the youth in Danville, Virginia based on The Bible.

Bee and Dan are a perfect match too. Their foundation is deep and unshakable like the concrete foundation of a skyscraper in New York City. It is a foundation of God, Jesus, and the Bible. Their relationship is beyond solid and Candy sees this. It makes her feel more and more comfortable with Ford.

Bee runs into their house for a quick shower. She had fun on the long bike ride home, but would much prefer to travel in their big truck and RV on long trips. Dan makes a critical mistake by parking his beloved flag-painted hog directly behind the garage door.

Dan notices that the three acre yard around the house needs mowing. He is hot and tired from a day of riding the hog. The sky is blue with puffy white clouds. The red and white barn is standing tall with the huge US flag waving in the breeze above the second floor barn doors. "Baba O'Riley" by the Who plays on the truck's stereo.

Dan carries his stuff into the house and uses the bathroom next to the kitchen. He flips through a pile of mail. He walks into the garage and opens the garage door. He puts the truck into reverse and punches the gas. He slams into the hog. He drags it six feet and then realizes what he has done.

"What an idiot! How can you be so stupid? What in the world have you done? Why did you do that? You are such a moron Dan," Dan said to himself.

The Wyatt bike is laying on the gravel driveway mangled. The front fender is bent upwards. Both sides of the fat bobs are dented. The exhaust pipes are scratched and bent. He is just staring at his huge mistake and wondering how he could be so dumb. The diesel truck is still running. "Roxanne" by the Police is playing in the truck.

Bee runs out of the garage after her quick shower and sees the damaged 2013 Harley Davidson Breakout. She heard the collision between the truck and the motorcycle from the kitchen. Dan is just standing there talking to himself. He is calling himself an idiot over and over.

She notices the handlebars broken into two pieces. The smell of gasoline is very strong. She sees her foot pegs laying five feet from the Harley. The turn and tail lights are smashed. The chrome is scratched beyond repair. She has floss wrapped around her finger.

"What did you do? It is okay, we have insurance baby. Do not worry. Do not worry. We can have it repaired. Come inside and eat this massive ribeye steak I grilled for you from Weis Markets. They have the best steak. I knew you were dumb when I married you," Bee said. She hugs her man and rubs his back to console him.

The hog is laying on its side on the gravel driveway. All of a sudden a fire starts. Gasoline poured all over the hot bike and the gravel driveway. It took a couple minutes to ignite.

Bee and Dan run away from the mangled bike and just watch it burn. He thinks about the end of the Easy Rider movie and the flag bike burning beside the country road in Mississippi. He was surprised at the tragic ending to the classic biker movie. He always thought it was kind of a dumb ending for a biker movie to kill the bikers and destroy the choppers.

He imagines a drone filming his hog and rising up into the sky above their farm just like the camera man in the helicopter did in 1969 on the movie set. At least nobody was killed or injured in this horrible accident down on the farm. He hears the Roger McGuinn song "The Ballad of Easy Rider" coming from the truck.

"Well, I guess it is no big deal. Our deductible is only $250. Everyone makes mistakes. I need to get the mother load out," Dan said with a smile. He walks behind the house to get a hose to put out the fire.

About the Author

David Xu was born in Danville, VA and has lived in Apopka, FL, Salisbury, NC, Harrisburg, PA, and Ashland, PA. He was in the U.S. Army (active and reserve) for thirty years, taught community college business courses, and was self employed in IT. He earned an MBA from James Madison University. He and his wife Nancy enjoy family, friends, airplanes, Harley-Davidson motorcycles, walking, recreational vehicles, reading, bicycles, ducks, geese, and traveling. Their favorite TV show is Seinfeld and saw him live in August 2019 in Reading (great show). David loves rock and roll music, concerts, and documentaries. Lynyrd Skynyrd and Ted Nugent are his favorite artists. His favorite book is Guns, Germs, and Steel by Jared Diamond.

Contact Information:
Dave224422@yahoo.com

www.ingramcontent.com/pod-product-compliance
Lightning Source LLC
LaVergne TN
LVHW091536060526
838200LV00036B/636